Quinter

C. REYNOLDS KELLER

Quinter, LLC
dba Quinter Publications
Chagrin Falls, Ohio

Primary ISBN 978-0-9847898-0-1
ePUB 978-0-9847898-1-8
ePDF 978-0-9847898-2-5

Printed in the United States of America
www.quinter.biz

First Edition

CONTENTS

To Carrie, Sarah, Chauncey, and Joe with enduring pride and affection

Quinter

C. REYNOLDS KELLER

1

THE OFFER

DEEP IN THOUGHT AFTER LUNCH with his old classmate David Bordman at Café Angeles on West Sixth Street, Thomas March Quinter walked through the Terminal Tower lobby toward the elevators. Tom had been surprised that Nortex, the huge defense contractor where Bordman was a rising star, had offered to pay him a good deal of money to set up corporate sites on the Costa del Sol during what promised to be a very nice paid vacation.

Nodding to Alex at the security desk, Quinter stepped on the elevator and punched the number of his floor. When the elevator door opened on seven, he was startled by a cry coming from the direction of his office at the end of the hall. Unnerved, he broke into a trot down the narrow corridor. When he was within feet of the opened door to his office, he noticed the broken lock.

Without warning, the door flew wide, grazing his chest and stopping him in his tracks. For a brief second, he stood face to face with a powerfully built, swarthy man with disheveled black hair and a bushy moustache. The man drove his right forearm into Quinter's right cheek. Dazed, Quinter fell backward into the wall striking the left side of his head against the unforgiving marble surface. As he struggled to regain his senses, the man fled down the corridor and into the stairwell.

Quinter staggered into the reception room of his office. Furniture was upended, and books and documents were scattered everywhere—and Jennifer, his secretary, was crouched on her hands and knees, whimpering, and struggling to get up.

He ran to her and knelt, trying to comprehend what he was seeing as his eyes fastened on the growing pool of blood on the tan carpet beneath her head. The right shoulder of her stone-washed blue denim dress was torn, and there were deep crimson gouges in the exposed flesh.

"Jennifer, my God, Jennifer, you're hurt!" he cried, raising her head toward him and exposing the nasty gash on the left side of her mouth.

"I think I'm OK. Oh Tom . . .," she sobbed, her body heaving with every word.

Quinter helped her to a sitting position on the floor, picked up the telephone, and hammered the number for security. "Alex, this is Quinter. Some son of a bitch beat up Jennifer, and trashed my office. Couldn't have been two minutes ago. He's stocky, dark complexion, thick black hair. Moustache. He headed for the north stairwell of the seventh floor. Get the bastard."

"Stay there, Tom," said Alex in a calm professional tone, "we'll get on it and I'll call EMS."

Quinter helped Jennifer to the receptionist chair. Hurriedly, he retrieved a wet washcloth from the adjoining restroom and brought it to her, watching as she applied the cloth to her swollen mouth, her shoulders now heaving only sporadically and the flow of blood slowing to a trickle.

2

Quinter surveyed the scene more carefully. The couch was overturned and books had been randomly torn from the shelves lining the reception area. Papers and literature from loose-leaf notebooks had been strewn throughout the room, and the walnut coffee table upended.

"What happened, Jenny?"

"Tom . . ., it was awful. I came back from shopping and I heard several crashes as I approached the office. I could see the lock had been smashed, and the door was open. I should have stopped right there and gone down to Security, but I walked in to see what was going on, and that's when he grabbed me and threw me against the desk. And then he . . . he hit me. Oh god, Tom," Jennifer broke down again, just as the EMS team arrived accompanied by Alex and another security officer.

"We'll take care of things now, sir," said one of the paramedics. "This young lady is going to need a couple of sutures. We will take you to the St. Joseph's Emergency room, ma'am." Turning to Quinter, he said, "You can meet her there."

Alex said, "It's a damn shame, Tom. I've reported the matter to the Cleveland police, and they say they will look into it. If you're alright, I'll go check up on things."

"I'm alright, thanks for your help, Alex."

Just as Alex departed, Ralph Barnes, Quinter's young associate, appeared. "What in god's name happened?" he asked.

"It's a nasty story," said Quinter slumping into the receptionist's chair. "I'll tell you later. See what you can do about the library. I'll take care of the rest."

"You OK, Boss?"

Quinter nodded. Barnes, sensing Quinter wanted to be alone, shrugged his shoulders and headed toward the library.

Quinter leaned back in the chair and, as he closed his eyes, his mind wandered back to earlier that morning when he sat at his desk, puffing discontentedly on a Macanudo cigar.

IT WAS A beautiful late August morning and the sunlight streamed through the leaded glass, revealing the necessary legal clutter surrounding Tom. Now that he had completed the first draft of the brief, an array of papers and opened law books needed organization and re-shelving, but the task was too formidable to start at the moment. He looked out across Cleveland's Public Square.

From the seventh floor of the Terminal Tower, he could almost make out the faces of the passers-by. His thoughts strayed to the faces of the jury as they had returned to report the verdict yesterday. Those faces were all too recognizable— stern and foreboding.

"Guilty of second degree burglary," the foreman intoned. *Guilt by association*, Quinter thought at the time while uncomfortably noting his client appeared relieved at being convicted of the lesser charge. The five thousand dollar fee, however, would be helpful. If only he could now collect the last fifteen hundred.

The days of high stakes trial poker at Davis-James seemed a distant memory.

Good old Davis-James, he thought. *Twenty five hundred hours and a cloud of dust!*

When he was invited to join the firm—as the youngest partner in fifteen years—the event was the product of skillful politics, hard work, and a bit of good luck. The firm pace had been great for his career, but intolerable for his wife, Natalie, who had divorced him a year ago in the fall of 1986. And, of course, there had been Jennifer.

IT WAS EARLY summer 1968. Quinter was fresh out of law school and ready to take on the world, or so he thought. There being no such thing as "time-off" in those days, Quinter went straight from high school to college to law school to the practice of law.

He will never forget his big-time Davis-James interview.

The elevator to the twenty-first floor of the Huntington Building seemed to take forever. Finally, it jerked to a stop, startling him. The door creaked open slowly and he edged his way into the expansive and elegantly appointed reception room. There was no mistaking his final destination—a large plaque spelled out the name in ornate bronze letters. D A V I S-J A M E S. An oil painting framed in Elizabethan gold leaf hanging above the receptionist's desk depicted a stern-faced man, his white goatee crisply shaped to a fine point, wearing a bow-tie, and glaring off into the distance. His left hand held a place in the leather-bound book perched on the edge of a wooden table next to him. A small bronze placard written in cursive letters identified the gentleman as "Emmet Wiley James, 1883-1963."

In contrast to the solemn portrait, the sleekly dressed receptionist, her red hair tied back by a green ribbon, was frantically attempting to accommodate a myriad of flashing yellow lights on the Bakelite console spread out before her. As if on cue, the lights disappeared, and the receptionist, drawing a deep breath, looked up at a young man she judged to be about six feet tall approaching her from the elevator bank.

She saw him staring at the bronze letters, struggling to become comfortable with the intimidating space, but only momentarily thrown-off by the surroundings. He gathered himself and walked without hurry, directly toward her.

"Hello. Tom Quinter to meet with Mr. Davis. And yes, I do have an appointment." Quinter smiled at the young woman.

"Certainly, Mr. Quinter. I'll tell him you're here. Would you like some coffee?"

"Thanks," said Quinter, "but I'm all coffeed out."

Nathan Davis, Cleveland's foremost corporate attorney, head of the Growth Association, and son of the founder, looked up from the single sheet of paper he was holding and shifted his gaze to Quinter who was standing on the other side of his immense mahogany desk. The young lawyer did not seem nervous, a quality Mr. Davis found to be unusual. His short blond hair, which apparently had just been combed, was still damp in places and was already becoming mildly disheveled.

"Well, Mr. Quinter," intoned Mr. Davis while adjusting his black bow tie, "please have a seat. I see you finally made it into the upper third of your graduating class at Princeton—but not until the last semester of your senior year?" Davis raised his eyebrows in mock surprise.

"That's correct, Mr. Davis." Quinter's gray eyes betrayed nothing of his emotional state, which bordered on controlled terror. Somehow, he knew the old buzzard would get right to the worst.

Hearing no explanation, Davis pressed on. "Davis-James is one of this nation's established law firms, Mr. Quinter. 'White shoe,' if you will. We have the luxury of being choosey. Top third, and at the last moment, Mr. Quinter?"

Quinter shifted in his chair. He focused on the words "white shoe," a term traditionally reserved for the most elite New York Wall Street law firms—even while thinking Davis was probably a supercilious son of a bitch.

"It was a tough year for my family, Mr. Davis. My parents were divorced, and I spent some time at home with my mother." Having found the appropriate response, Quinter's feelings of anxiety seemed to vanish as if by magic. The candor of the reply caused Davis's thin white lips to part in a smile, which he suppressed. The young man clearly had a sense of balance and presence . . . and he might even be telling the truth.

"I notice you did somewhat better at Michigan law—but no Law Review?" Davis continued, now looking out the window through the bright sunshine toward white-capped blue Lake Erie.

"No, sir. But I did place first in Moot Court competition," answered Quinter.

"So, you want to be a trial lawyer? From time to time I do have use for a litigator in my own practice, Mr. Quinter, but only when all reasonable avenues have been exhausted. A messy business. Messy, but necessary." His dislike of the process was evident in his voice although his recognition of huge litigation fees was not.

Sensing no immediate response was necessary, Quinter sat back slightly in his chair. In a single motion he slipped his hand across his blue and red striped rep tie, under his charcoal gray suit jacket, and pulled a cigarette from the pack in his shirt pocket.

"We do have litigation here at Davis-James, Mr. Quinter. And some rather good trial attorneys. In fact, we have a number of former trial judges."

Quinter lit the cigarette, placing the extinguished match in the unused crystal ashtray on the corner of Davis's desk. He looked up casually, searching for Davis's reaction, and noticing none, offered a careful response. "I've heard that, Mr. Davis. And that's why I want to work for your firm. I want to learn from the best people and work on the most interesting cases."

Davis smiled as fully as he was capable. He could not help but feel a twinge of admiration for Quinter's audacity. There was little doubt the cool-headed young man had some potential as a lawyer, and most assuredly, he was well on his way to mastering the game of intellectual chess.

"Well, Mr. Quinter, I do have another appointment. Thank you for coming. We will be in touch."

Davis arose from his chair and started toward the heavy walnut paneled door twenty-five feet away. Quinter followed, until Davis paused at the closed door, extending his hand. Quinter, caught by surprise, shifted the smoldering cigarette to his left hand, and shook hands firmly with Davis.

"Doris will show you out, Mr. Quinter," said Davis, opening the door and gesturing toward a white-haired woman sitting at a nearby desk. "and you may use the ashtray if you would like. Doris, please show Mr. Quinter the way, and when you come back, get my daughter, Natalie, on the phone."

"Of course, Mr. Davis," Doris responded from her desk, snapping to attention.

Quinter glanced uncomfortably at the long ash precariously perched on the end of his spent cigarette and then at the intricate pattern of the red Ziegler oriental area rug at his feet. Turning, he walked for what seemed like an eternity across Davis's office, and flicked the ash into the crystal ashtray, carefully putting out the remains. He then exchanged a now uncomfortable nodding good-bye with Davis.

Smiling slightly with relief, Quinter followed Doris down a long corridor, past the numerous offices, and occasional secretarial bays. After about a hundred feet, she turned left into another corridor. Now and then Quinter saw a young lawyer intently studying or writing, and there was always the busy secretary typing a document on her IBM Selectric. Doris and Quinter reached the end of the hall, passing the open doors of a large conference room in which half a dozen people in their shirtsleeves were studying documents piled high on a long conference table. She opened the door to the reception area, allowing Quinter to precede her.

"Thanks, Doris," Quinter offered pleasantly. "I've enjoyed the visit."

Doris, nodding, watched Quinter walk assuredly across the reception area. As if sensing that his confidence had begun to dissolve, she called out to him, "Mr. Quinter, Mr. Quinter!"

Quinter stopped.

"He likes you, Mr. Quinter, I can tell."

"Thanks, Doris. I think this firm has some good people and I know I've met two of them," he said, smiling at the red-headed receptionist who returned his smile. "Take care, now."

As QUINTER AGAIN focused upon the array of legal papers and open law books that needed organization and re-shelving, he was startled from his reverie by the keying of the intercom.

"Tom, a Mr. David Bordman called you earlier this morning and asked if he could meet you for lunch today. He can be reached at Stouffer's Hotel."

Quinter was surprised. "Thanks Jennifer," he said, and the intercom clicked off. He took a long puff on the Macanudo.

Bordman. David Marshall Bordman. Captain of Princeton's 1965 championship track team, a near miss for a Rhodes scholarship, and Quinter's commanding officer in NROTC. While Quinter had always thought Bordman a bit shallow, there was no arguing with his success. After graduating from Princeton, Bordman spent three years in Vietnam assigned to Naval Intelligence in Saigon, where he served as an information officer to the press. After his return to the States in 1969, he received an appointment to the CIA in a "publicly unspecified capacity." Eight years later, in 1977, he joined the Department of State as an Under Secretary for Spanish Affairs. According to the *Wall Street Journal*, "Bordman resigned his post at State to accept the Executive Vice President's job at Nortex in 1984."

Bordman and Quinter had never been close. The differences in their personalities and attitude toward life and people prevented real friendship. Bordman's manner was crisp, almost rude, and his demeanor that of a man who expected results and would not tolerate failure. Quinter, on the other hand, was more relaxed and, as a consequence, often underestimated both as advocate and adversary. Where Bordman attacked by frontal assault, Quinter approached with calculation and understatement. Nonetheless, a certain begrudging respect plus their personal history had produced a relationship that was more than an acquaintanceship, yet one without warmth. For the first decade after college, they would get together when Quinter's practice took him to the nation's capital. Both serious young men, they often skipped happy hour in favor of a good workout in State's well-equipped gym. While Quinter found Bordman a bit too competitive, he had no trouble staying with him—and on occasion outdid him, usually just for the fun of it.

Quinter had seen Bordman only a few times since their fifteenth reunion in Princeton in 1980. At the reunion on Friday evening, they met by chance on McCosh Walk behind Brown and decided to circle up campus in order to walk through Blair Arch down the steps to the 15th Reunion tent in Henry/'01 Courtyard. At the tent, they grabbed a beer and reminisced over the 1965 NCAA track championship in which Quinter won second place in the broad jump, and Bordman captured gold in the 100-yard dash.

The rambling conversation then turned to Quinter's 1968 Saigon trip. After Quinter served three months of sea duty on a destroyer in the South China Sea, the ship made port in Saigon allowing Quinter the chance to get together with Bordman. They spent four debaucherous days of shore leave in Saigon, during which they drank too much and visited with 'ladies of the evening'. At the reunion, Quinter and Bordman, as if by unstated agreement, spoke little of their personal lives. They spent most of the time recounting college stories and later life experiences.

Quinter dialed Stouffer's, and asked for Bordman's room. Bordman picked up after a single ring.

"Hello, David, Tom Quinter. Long time no talk."

"Good morning, Tom. Appreciate you getting back. Can you meet me for lunch today? I have something I'd like to discuss with you."

"Of course, Dave. How about Stouffer's?"

"No," said Bordman with an emphasis that sounded out of place to Quinter. "Do you know the Cafe Angeles on West Sixth?"

"Sure," said Quinter, "I'll meet you at noon."

"Agreed," said Bordman. The line went dead.

Quinter gazed at the mahogany barometer clock that hung on the wall across the room from his desk. He had always loved barometers, and this was a beautiful one, a present from his mother on his 30th birthday. It was eleven o'clock and he noted with pleasure the ornate gold needle pointed to the center of the intricate "fair" symbol on the creamy pearl dial. He clicked the intercom.

"Jennifer, would you bring your book in for a minute?"

"Certainly," she replied.

Jennifer Millieux began working for Quinter two years before he resigned his partnership at Davis-James in December 1986. She had excellent secretarial skills and a reassuring way of dealing with clients and other lawyers. It was rumored in Davis-James partnership circles that an affair between Quinter and Millieux had resulted in Natalie's filing for divorce. But the claim was never brought out into the open. That was not the Davis-James way.

The door opened and Jennifer entered. A beautiful woman with dark, auburn hair and a full figure, she wore a stone-washed blue denim dress and her hair was tied back in a pony-tail.

"I'm sorry about the Bartlett matter," she said.

"Thanks. I appreciate your condolence. I'm not so sure that the man didn't bear some guilt. Fat chance we'll get the last fifteen hundred. Unless he wants an appeal. You certainly look lovely today."

"Thanks," she nodded unenthusiastically.

"Jennifer," Quinter continued, failing to acknowledge her demeanor, "I'm going to lunch with Dave Bordman. Would you call Jason and reserve a table for two at noon? Also, dun Bartlett's father for the money and tell him that I'll be speaking with him about the appeal early next week. And pretty please, dear Jennifer, do something about these damn books and papers. I'm going to Joe's for a haircut and then lunch at Cafe Angeles. I don't expect to return to the office before 2:30. Thanks."

As he had been speaking, Quinter had gotten up from his desk and began moving toward the door. He left the room speaking the last words over his shoulder, leaving Jennifer to deal with the problem.

"Damn," she said softly, *If he really thinks I look nice, he sure doesn't act like it.*

Quinter took the elevator to the tenth floor and walked briskly to the barbershop. As soon as he seated himself in the chair, Joe launched into a discussion of the Cleveland Brown's chances for Super Bowl contention, but Quinter's mind was elsewhere. He was confused by Bordman's call. It wasn't like Bordman to have wanted to see him on such short notice. Quinter hadn't seen or heard from him in several years and something about Bordman's tone made him uneasy.

Switching the subject to basketball, Joe droned on, "Well you understand, Tom, any idiot would have known that Thompson wasn't worth trading a second and a ninth round for . . . should I raise the sides a little?"

"Sure," replied Quinter.

Later, after tipping Joe two dollars, he took the elevator to the Terminal Tower Lobby. Nodding to his friend Alex, chief of Tower City Security, Quinter walked out the front entrance into the bright sunshine of Public Square.

Deciding to take the scenic route to Cafe Angeles, he walked the Northeast diagonals across Public Square past the fountain. A large sign in bold red letters read: "DANGER! DO NOT WADE. CHEMICALS ADDED." Quinter recalled the children playing in the fountain at the foot of Boulevard St. Michel in Paris, smiling at the remembered laughter, and he thought *Fountains should be played in— especially by kids.*

He wondered about Natalie and what she was doing. After the divorce he attempted to salvage a friendship. It was good to make the effort and, essential for the well-being of their son. Natalie, an investment banker, had scheduled a business trip to Saudi Arabia after Labor Day and the young man was to stay with Quinter for two weeks before starting his upper middle year at Exeter. Quinter was fiercely proud of his son, who had exhibited ability in track to which he in his younger years could only aspire. He was also scholarly, having made the Headmaster's list for the second consecutive quarter last year.

Quinter was startled from his thoughts by the sound of a blaring horn.

"Why don't you watch where you're going, pal?"

Quinter leaped for the safety of the curb, and yelled, "Screw you, friend" at the departing vehicle.

It was quarter of twelve as he arrived at the door of Cafe Angeles. Jason greeted him warmly.

"I have a quiet table for you, Mr. Quinter. Away from the bar, in the corner with the big window."

"Thanks Jason. How's Rita?"

"She's Rita," Jason shrugged, gesturing to the matronly-appearing lady ferociously tending customers at the bar.

"I'm expecting a Mr. Bordman," continued Quinter.

"He has already arrived, sir, and I have seated him at your table. Please." Jason gestured toward the table in the far corner next to the window while beginning to escort Quinter. As they neared the table, Quinter noticed that a man wearing a white prayer robe and a white skull cap sitting at the bar was looking toward him. The man's glance seemed to call for a sign of acknowledgment, so Quinter nodded politely, but the man averted his gaze.

"How are you, Dave? You're looking well," he began as he approached his former classmate.

"You too, Tom," Bordman replied, as the two men first looked closely at each other and then seated themselves. In fact, Bordman did look well. His coal black hair had grayed at the temples in a distinguished manner, and even though he had put on ten or fifteen pounds—which made Quinter wonder if his former classmate had relaxed his once-rigid workout routine—he carried the weight easily. He was wearing a dark blue pin-striped tailored suit, a Tattersall button down shirt, and a maroon tie in a paisley pattern. As he stood to greet Quinter, Bordman seemed sure of himself, but Quinter thought he detected a hint of ill-ease.

The two chatted about college days, Quinter's departure from Davis-James and his new law practice, and Bordman's new position at Nortex. Bordman began by telling him proudly how he was surprised and intrigued when Duane Johnson, the

14

Nortex Chairman, offered him the Executive Vice Presidency. Johnson had implied that Bordman could become president of the giant conglomerate within a short period of time if he could prove his ability to manage competently and be a consummate "team player".

Johnson had assigned Bordman the responsibility of negotiating a substantial arms deal with the Spanish Government. In fact, Bordman had just returned from Madrid where he had discussed the transaction with leading members of the Defense Ministry and Parliament.

"I and several other Nortex people will be spending a good deal of time in Spain over the next few months," said Bordman, "and I would like your help."

Quinter's eyes widened in surprise.

"I'm flattered, but why me?"

Most of the lunch crowd had evaporated, and Rita was in the final throes of clean-up. The man in the prayer robe was paying his bill and Quinter caught his glance as he walked slowly toward the door.

"The situation is delicate and you are someone I know I can trust, Tom," Bordman said with apparent sincerity. "Nortex will be moving a number of people to Spain; technicians, numbers people, political people. We'll need somewhere to stay—somewhere out of the limelight. I'd like us to stay down on the Costa del Sol—maybe near Malaga, an area as I recall, you know well."

Quinter hesitated, trying to recall when he would have told Bordman of his travels to Spain. He relaxed as he remembered their telephone conversation and that it had occurred in the proper chronological sequence after he had returned to the States. He refocused on Bordman's words.

"I'm sure it wouldn't be difficult for you to obtain a villa, some storage space, and a landing area for the helicopter—possibly a farm. It would need to be a safe area for us, and yet just a short flight from Madrid. Nortex will pay all expenses and a fee of eighteen hundred dollars a day. What do you say? Will you help me out?"

For the moment, Quinter kept his gaze on the checkered tablecloth. Eighteen hundred dollars a day? *Weeks* would pass when he didn't earn that much. Yes, the money sounded just fine. He could buy a new couch for the office. And new curtains. Jennifer had been bugging him to replace the curtains for months. And a full set of the Northeast Reporter, Second. But he remembered the editorial in the Plain Dealer criticizing Nortex for taking illegal contract profits and decided even though the money was good, to proceed cautiously.

"And the reason the matter is 'delicate' . . .?" he said, looking squarely into Bordman's ice-blue eyes.

"A number of folks think Spain's national interest does not require rearmament to the extent which we, well I mean NATO, believes to be necessary. And the profits, the profits to Nortex are, shall we say, substantial."

He continued. "We need a secure base of operations. I would prefer that the initial ground work be done by someone who has no ties to the company. What do you say? You ought to be able to do the whole assignment in a week or so, and," Bordman added, "the Spanish coast is beautiful this time of year."

His mind spinning, Quinter paused. "When do you need a decision? I have a law practice—and then there's my son. He was going to spend a couple of weeks with me after Labor Day."

"I need a decision by noon tomorrow," declared Bordman. "You should be back in time to meet with your boy, and if you are a little late he can always spend a day or so with his cousins

16

in Brecksville. He'll understand. Your associate, what's his name, Ralph, Ralph Barnes can cover emergencies."

The statement jarred Quinter. He knew he had never said anything to Bordman about his Brecksville cousins or about Barnes. And why the big rush? But Bordman's voice interrupted Quinter's thoughts.

"Tom, I realize this is precipitous and must seem hurried to you, but my instructions were to find a lawyer from the heartland, not an Easterner, a small firm or solo practitioner if possible with no ties to the company, who knew Spain, and someone we, and especially I, could trust. That's you, pure and simple. And a sudden shift in plans meant there was no time to waste. Hence the deadline. I'm sure you understand."

Bordman picked up the check, signaling that his part of this conversation was over. The two men walked from the Cafe into the bright afternoon sun. As they shook hands, Quinter said," I'll let you know by noon tomorrow."

"Noon tomorrow." repeated Bordman. "Call me at the hotel and if I'm not there leave a message: Yes or No."

"I will," said Quinter glancing at Bordman's back as he walked away. The idea was intriguing. *What could be the harm?* he thought. *First class travel at the expense of Nortex. . . It should be easy to rent a villa and a small farm at this time of year. And, of course, there is the money. . .*

He wondered if he dared to ask Jennifer to come with him, particularly since they had not been together for some time. But he knew she'd spent several summers with her father after he took a job in Mexico City, and spoke fluent Spanish. She would be a great help making travel arrangements and using the damn Spanish telephone system. Yes, he would ask her to go with him. *She might even agree, and it might be nice to have an attractive companion,* he thought.

17

He walked back along the same route across Public Square, past the fountain, and into the lobby of the Terminal Tower.

QUINTER PLACED HIS left hand on his throbbing cheek, gently probing, until he winced with pain when his fingers found the area that had absorbed the full force of the blow. He leaned forward in the chair, once again viewing the chaos of his reception room. Sitting with his elbows on his knees and his head in his hands, he cursed, "You miserable son of a bitch."

2

JENNIFER'S DECISION

B Y THE TIME QUINTER RETURNED to his office from Central Police Station, it was nearly 5:30. He'd had to wait several hours before the investigating officers took his statement, and the calm questioning of the detectives seemed interminable.

As Quinter began to right the upset furniture and shelve the legal books, he recounted the events of the day. Just as a song intrudes on the mind and maddeningly replays itself over and over again, his mind kept trying to find a connection between his unusual lunch conversation with Bordman and the intruder that afternoon. The overly curious man in the prayer robe at Cafe Angeles was an interesting sidelight, but the pieces didn't fit, for the simple reason there were not enough of them. Yet, the proximity in time of the two events continued to trouble him.

Quinter's uncertainty about the possibility of his own involvement complicated his assessment of possible danger to Jennifer. He had a vague yet fleeting sense of guilt that the attack might be the result of some client's misplaced anger. But regardless of the reason, he was determined this would not happen again.

Momentarily surprised by his protective feelings for Jennifer, he decided, on the spot, to offer to take her to his new apartment on the east side of Cleveland, just north of Shaker Square.

At 6:30 that evening, Quinter parked his newly-leased Lexus in the St. Joseph's Hospital parking lot. After waiting for an ambulance to pass, he walked toward the Emergency Room, and entered the admitting area where two middle-aged women were seated at the information counter. Although there was no one in line ahead of him, it didn't look to Quinter as if the women were doing any work, yet it took several attempts before he gained the attention of one of them.

"Ms. Jennifer Millieux, please." There was no response.

"Excuse me, where is Ms. Millieux?"

The woman raised her head, but said nothing.

"I am looking for Ms. Jennifer Millieux. Can you tell me where to find her?"

"Room three. Down the hall. Left." After delivering her response in a flat, begrudging manner, the woman returned her gaze to the blotter in front of her. Annoyed, Quinter turned toward the hallway.

The odor of disinfectant was strong as he opened the door of room number three and saw Jennifer propped up in bed dressed in a white hospital gown. She did not notice him for a moment, but when she did, she turned her face toward him, attempting a weak smile that was cut short by a burst of pain. She winced as she spoke.

"Hi, Tom."

"You don't look so hot," he said noting the angry red swelling on the right side of her face, and immediately regretting his less-than-thoughtful statement.

20

"I don't hurt so much anymore." she said. "When will I be able to get out?"

"Pretty soon," he replied evenly.

A minute later, a young intern appeared. In a halting, still new, bedside manner he announced, "You're free to go. The wound is clean and it shouldn't scar. By the way, we used a new type of suture which doesn't require removal. The subcutaneous portion will dissolve and the part exposed to the air will simply fall out."

Jennifer felt relieved, and, looking at the doorway, saw that the nurse had returned. She was carrying a paper bag that contained Jennifer's clothes and personal items. Her blue denim dress had been torn and stained with dried dark blood in several places. With the assistance of the nurse, she walked behind the screen and put on her shoes and the green hospital scrubs which she'd been given to go home. She discarded her dress in a waste receptacle. Then, with Quinter's support, she walked unevenly down the corridor toward the parking lot.

"I'm going to take you to my place for the night, Jenny. Please don't disagree. Also I have some more information to tell you."

She nodded weakly.

On the drive to his apartment, Quinter related, in detail, his conversation with Bordman, as well as his past history with the man. He told her that he had already determined to accept Bordman's offer. To his disappointment, however, when he asked her to accompany him, she said she would have to think about it.

QUINTER'S SECOND FLOOR apartment was similar to others belonging to bachelors in their early forties, but neater than most. A dark brown overstuffed sofa, his grand-mother's sitting chair, and his favorite, an amber-colored recliner furnished the fair-sized living room, furniture he'd obtained when he and Natalie separated. An octagonal mirror with a red oak frame which he had purchased at a garage sale and rebuilt from scratch hung on the wall opposite two pairs of windows. At the point where the frame met the silvered glass, he had stuffed various notes and cards which seemed important at the time. To the left of the windowed wall a large 26 inch screen television sat on a table.

Jennifer followed Quinter through the living room, pausing to look at the striking water color hanging on the wall behind the recliner. The painting was of a rugged Maine Seascape, the shore holding firm against the onslaught of a Nor'easter. "I bought that last year when I visited Jeff Downing and his wife, Martha, at their summer home in Gloucester." he offered. "I roomed with Jeff my senior year at Michigan Law in 1968. He's been a good friend."

"It's a strong painting, Tom. I can almost hear the roar of the wind." Jennifer answered. "Are you and Jeff still close?"

"Yes, and we've kept in touch over the years. After graduation, he joined Swarthmore and Wesley in Boston, a big, prestigious firm. Close to two hundred lawyers today. He made partner in a little less than seven years, probably because of his growing reputation in international law. Upon Wesley's recommendation, the State Department asked him to head the U.S. team," Quinter continued, despite noticing that Jennifer's attention was flagging, "which tried to negotiate the boundary dispute between Honduras and Nicaragua. Never happened because the Nicaraguans became furious when the U.S. began supporting the Contras, but Jeff distinguished himself."

"Interesting." Jennifer replied although it was clear she no longer wanted conversation.

"You'd like him. His wife Martha is a sweetheart," Quinter continued. Then, gesturing toward the bedroom, he took her hand and led her into the room.

"You'll be comfortable here. I'm going to order something to eat. How's pizza sound, or maybe chicken soup?" Before Jennifer could answer, Quinter left the room leaving the door slightly ajar.

Jennifer seated herself on the king-sized bed just as a wave of exhaustion rolled over her. She looked around the room. She thought it felt comfortable. The walls were freshly painted light yellow, and white lace curtains adorned the windows at the head and right side of the bed. Several framed posters by French Impressionists hung in a step-like pattern on the walls opposite and to the left of the bed.

The bedside table and bureau were matched mahogany with burnished brass fittings, and the white bedspread complemented the curtains. A light brown oval carpet covered almost the entire floor and a refinished antique rocker sat in the corner. Yes, she thought, she'd be quite comfortable here for the night.

A she lay down on the bed, the events of the day spinning around in her head, she wondered why she'd accepted Quinter's invitation to spend the night, seeing as they had not been intimate for some time. Rather than delve into a mixed bag of emotions, she simply concluded that it must have been because she'd been hurt and needed a safe haven.

IN A HALF-DREAM, her mind went back to a cold snowy day in February 1984, three and one-half years earlier.

She was hurrying up Euclid Avenue, toward Ninth, and when she passed the bleached walls of the National City Bank Building, she was dismayed to see from the Ameritrust Clock across the street that she was already five minutes late. *Damn*, she thought, as she pushed the revolving doors of the Union Commerce Building. As soon as she spun her way through the turning door, she felt reassured by the warmth, and stopped at the directory.

"Davis . . . Davis . . . Davis," she repeated until her eyes found the word. Davis-James, twenty-first floor. Looking at her reflection in the glass of the directory, she thought her hair seemed out of place, her navy blue suit disheveled, and her Louis Vuitton purse didn't match. As she removed the scarf and attempted to shake her shoulder-length hair into place, Jennifer worried that she would not make a good impression.

She glanced around, and observing no one nearby, snatched her comb from the clashing purse. She gave her hair three or four quick strokes before quitting in frustration and turning, walked defiantly toward the elevator bank.

Entering the law firm of Davis-James, Jennifer was oblivious to the ornate traditional surroundings of the reception area. She walked directly to the receptionist behind the desk and said, "I'm Jennifer Millieux, and I have an appointment with a Mrs. Greenleaf."

Half an hour later, Doris Greenleaf studied the Bernot Typing Test results in her trademark methodical manner honed over a hundred previous occasions. She displayed only the mildest surprise at finding one error had been made at a typing speed of one hundred ten words a minute.

"This is good work," Doris Greenleaf said, as much to herself as to the young woman seated in front of her. "I'll see if Mr. Quinter is available now, Jennifer. He's one of Mr. Davis's favorites, and I might say, the only one of this elite group who's involved in litigation. Mr. Davis likes corporate and tax people. He says they are much more predictable. But I think you would enjoy working for Mr. Quinter. He's a good lawyer and a fine person. He has a heavy work load and needs someone with good skills. I think he will like you."

"I hope so. Thank you, Mrs. Greenleaf. You're very kind."

"Miss Greenleaf, honey," replied Doris, with a smile, as she dialed Quinter's number. "Mr. Quinter, Miss Jennifer Millieux is here. I'll bring her down now if that's alright."

Damned 'Dead Man's Statute', thought Quinter, slamming shut a heavy law book. *One man is dead and the law presumes the other one is a liar. Poor policy.* Not only did it make his case more difficult to prove, it meant that the trial preparation would be much more expensive. Quinter's mind assessed the legal possibilities before concluding, with a touch of anger, that the expense bothered him the most. "We simply have to do something," he said aloud.

Quinter, although slightly startled by the knock on the door, was immediately impressed: Jennifer Millieux was one of the most attractive women he'd ever seen. Her dark navy suit subtly accentuated the curves of her full body, and her brown eyes sparkled with life and energy. Within minutes, Quinter found himself confiding in her about his plans for upcoming trials and his vague but relentless dissatisfaction with his present position.

"I don't know what I can offer you, Jennifer, except I can promise you will never be bored. Also, the pay is pretty good."

Jennifer looked at Quinter, noting that his broad shoulders were tipped forward while he appealed to her with what she believed was sincerity. He was now looking directly at her and their eyes met. The intensity of his gaze made it momentarily difficult to follow his words, but, gradually and without realizing it, she became content just to be the center of his attention. She felt a warmth flicker over her—until it was chilled by a glimpse of the beautiful blond woman in the picture frame on the credenza behind his desk.

"So, Jennifer," Quinter concluded after a careful explanation of the demands of trial work, "I don't know where I will be in three or four years. But if you want the job, I am offering it to you."

"I can start in two weeks, Mr. Quinter," Jennifer replied immediately.

J ENNIFER BLINKED AS she reconnected with her present surroundings and her eyes came to rest upon the white lace draperies in Quinter's bedroom.

Should I accept Quinter's offer to accompany him to Spain to scout for this Nortex Company, she wondered. Other than the summers of her second and third year which she spent with her father in Mexico City, she had never traveled outside the United States. This was a trip to Spain, to the Costa del Sol. She had heard the guarded excitement in Quinter's voice as he talked about his conversation with Bordman. *Perhaps it would be an exciting adventure to share,* she thought, *and it is high time to find out if this man is interested or even capable of sharing with me again. Yes, I will do it.*

She smiled to herself. Several minutes later, when Quinter knocked on the door carrying two slices of cheese pizza for her, she was fast asleep.

Sitting back in the corner of the sofa with his feet on the coffee table, Quinter washed the last of the pizza down with a large gulp of water. His mind returned to Bordman's proposition. He had decided to give Bordman a call. But first, he had another job to do.

He rose from the sofa and walked over to the hall closet. From behind his old Ghee karate fighting jacket and under his yellow, green, and brown belts, he withdrew a well-preserved leather shoulder holster and six magazines each loaded with eight rounds. After laying out the items he unsnapped the 7.65 mm Mauser pistol, setting it on the table. Grasping the slide, he cocked the weapon several times and then removed the firing pin from a small oil cloth wrapping, reinstalling it with a soft snick. He would be ready for any new attack.

Quinter was good with a handgun, but he was an excellent shot with a rifle. When he was fifteen his parents sent him to a summer camp in Pennsylvania's Allegheny Mountains. Despite a nasty reoccurrence of childhood asthma he became the camp's starting shortstop and he learned to shoot. He discovered that he was a natural marksman and had little difficulty learning the names and operation of the single shot .22 caliber Stevens rifle. By the time the camp session ended, he had earned Sharpshooter rank and several bars. A few years later he mastered the M-1 jungle carbine his uncle had salvaged from a barge loaded down with a half-million of the weapons just before the vessel was scuttled in the Pacific at the end of World War II.

Quinter's fondness for rifles was matched by his dislike for pistols. "Any damn fool can kill with a pistol," he liked to say, "and he usually kills himself or a friend." Quinter cocked the Mauser and pulled the trigger, hearing the clean crack of metal against metal as the hammer struck home. He had won the Mauser in a poker game during his last night of active duty aboard the destroyer as she lay at anchor in San Francisco Bay. The half-drunk lieutenant had the misfortune to call, backed by the Mauser, Quinter's three kings. Once the weapon had changed hands, Quinter set out to learn it just as he had the old Stevens.

After a short pause to admire the machining and engineering of the gun, Quinter checked the clips and fastened one of them into each of the four leather compartments on the holster belt. Then, carefully grasping the silencer, he fit it into its place on the belt, replaced the remaining two clips beneath the karate belts behind the Ghee, and hung the holster and gun on a hook at the back of the closet.

Now for Brother Dave, he thought, as he pushed the necessary buttons on the phone. Bordman answered on the second ring.

"I've been considering your proposal, Dave, and I've decided I'll take the job."

"That's great, Tom," Bordman replied.

"One condition, however," Quinter continued, "I've asked my secretary, Jennifer Millieux to go with me. She's fluent in Spanish. If she accepts, I will have additional expenses."

"Of course," Bordman answered, and Quinter was relieved to hear no hint of sarcasm or surprise in his voice. "You will both have to be ready to leave by 6:00 tomorrow night. Can you manage it, Tom?"

"We can," he replied.

"Good. I want to take you up to corporate headquarters in Haverhill—that's in Massachusetts in case you've forgotten your New England geography after all your years in Ohio—and introduce you to some Nortex people. Oh, and Tom, do you and your secretary have valid passports?"

"I do," said Quinter, "but I'm not sure about Jennifer."

"We can take care of any problem. I'll meet you at the Flight Services gate at Lakefront Airport tomorrow at 6:00 pm sharp. Night, Tom. I know you will be a lot of help."

After he'd hung up, Quinter walked through the living room to the bedroom. Through its partially-opened door, he could see, in the glow of the bathroom light, that Jennifer was in bed and, apparently, sleeping heavily. Tip-toeing past the sleeping woman on his way to the bathroom, Quinter paused for a moment to glance at her.

Once inside the bathroom, Quinter thought about how good it would feel to take a shower, but, realizing the noise might wake her up, he turned off the light, and returned to the living room. From the packed linen closet, he pulled a pillow and two down comforters. Back in the bedroom, he placed one of the comforters over Jennifer. In the living room, he stripped to his underwear, lay down on the sofa, pulled the other comforter over himself, and was asleep in seconds.

3

LAVENDER FOR A PARTY

THE SLEEK NORTEX GATES LEARJET banked awkwardly against the stiff northeast wind as it turned toward final approach to runway two four at Cleveland Lakefront airport. At the last instant before touchdown, the captain kicked in the correct amount of left rudder to straighten the nose to runway heading, and brought the craft to a smooth landing. He maneuvered the aircraft off the active runway at the first high speed taxiway, and then began a slow taxi toward the private gate, as the co-pilot flipped the switches retracting the flaps and speed brakes.

Eyes averted from the low evening sun, Quinter looked out across the field and toward Lake Erie beyond. The lake was rough, the water inside the piled stone breakwall churning with a thousand surges erupting high into the air. He glanced at Jennifer, but his observation was interrupted by Bordman's crisp comment,

"It's time. We're pushing 6:30."

"Lead on," said Quinter.

As the trio walked through the main airport waiting area, Quinter noticed a slender, middle-aged man in a suit standing by the windows overlooking the tarmac. He had obviously been watching the arrival of the Nortex plane, but then transferred his attention to Quinter, until he realized that Quinter saw him. He then lowered his head and glanced at his newspaper. Quinter looked at him several times as he and Jennifer followed Bordman toward a glass door with the red decal "PILOTS ONLY".

When Quinter reached the door, the man looked up from his paper and their eyes met. Quinter smiled and nodded his head, but the man gave no reply. Instead, he placed the paper under his arm, picked up his brief case, and started away from the windows.

Once outside, the group walked heads down, against the strong wind, toward the lowering stairs of the jet. "NORTEX" was emblazoned in red across its tail. The handrail snapped into place and a young co-pilot dressed in a navy-blue uniform greeted them. The name NORTEX was woven in red on his left chest, and a gold insignia of two standing men, struggling with each other, was embossed on his right shoulder. "Good evening," he said as he smiled pleasantly.

"Good evening," replied Jennifer. Bordman grunted a bare acknowledgement.

Quinter took a last ground level look at the large glass windows of the airport lobby as he ascended the boarding steps, and saw the man in the suit framed in the center window, looking out across the tarmac toward the departing group. This time, however, the man did not avoid Quinter's gaze, and the two men measured one another until Quinter went through the open cabin door.

The aft seats of the plane were comfortably arranged around a small table made of polished teak. Forward, there were three rows of plush maroon seats, which could swivel inward to face one another. A bar adjacent to the bulkhead separated the cockpit from the passenger's cabin. The overall impression was one of graceful utility. *Very tasteful*, Quinter thought to himself.

"Please fasten your seatbelts and we'll be off in a minute," said the co-pilot as he disappeared into the cockpit.

Quinter and Jennifer walked toward the back of the plane and sat at the table across from Bordman.

"I think you'll enjoy this trip," began Bordman. "It's about two hours to Haverhill and an additional half hour by car to the headquarters. Johnson is giving a party at his home this evening to which you are invited. A number of Nortex people will be there. It will be a good way for you to meet the company."

The noise of the engines accelerating to take-off power cut Bordman short. Quinter looked at Jennifer. Her facial swelling was already beginning to recede and was being replaced by a yellowish black and blue oval which extended from the corner of her mouth to her right cheekbone. Quinter winced.

At two thousand feet, the pilot throttled back to a steady power climb as the aircraft pierced the tops of the broken clouds. Quinter looked out the window behind him to the northwest. The view was magnificent, with clouds of every color from a brilliant yellow to deep purple, slashed by long curved streaks of red-orange. Off-shore the lake was azure fading to a light blue-green at the shoreline. Rows of white caps were everywhere, crashing into and over the breakwall. Inside, choppy surges were a dark and angry green.

"You'll meet several people tonight who are involved in this NATO-sponsored sale to Spain," said Bordman in an attention-commanding tone. "One of them is Cornelius Tester whom we hired away from Madison and Company in Washington a little over a year ago. Korny acted as a troubleshooter for some of the tobacco companies up on the Hill ensuring their position was correctly presented. Graduated from Cornell, I believe, and spent a couple of years with an advertising agency in New York. He's in charge of the company's Public Information Department." Bordman pushed the overhead button for assistance. "And Graham Butler," he continued, "Graham received a promotion from his present position as Assistant Chief of Security to head of security for the Spanish venture. Accommodating fellow. Has a son at Exeter, a freshman, if I recall correctly."

The male attendant arrived in response to Bordman's call. "Can I help you, sir?"

"Absolute on the rocks, no fruit."

"Of course, sir. Would either of you like something?" he said, turning toward Quinter and Jennifer. After both declined, he left, heading toward the bar at the front of the aircraft.

Bordman leaned back in his seat, closed his eyes for a moment, and then continued. "Joel Johnson, the Chairman's son, will coordinate manufacture and delivery of the weapons. We're talking primarily about Aegis anti-aircraft rockets, Agena anti-tank missiles, M-16 automatic rifles, and supporting munitions and parts. But you don't need to remember all the details. Just light weapons and rockets.

"Joel will be there tonight. He's young, graduated from Harvard, last year. Very bright and the apple of his father's eye, but young as I said . . ."

As Bordman's voice trailed off, Quinter noticed the edge of scorn in the words. The attendant returned with Bordman's vodka. He took a drink immediately, and then dismissed the attendant with a quick wave of his hand.

"Sir Bertram Reynolds," Bordman continued, "the President of our British shipping subsidiary, has been tapped to head the venture. He's an intriguing individual, smart and knowledgeable, although too academic for my taste. Has a lot of highly-placed Spanish friends."

With scarcely a break in transition, Bordman finished his drink, sighed, and closed his eyes. A few seconds later, his chin dropped to his chest, and he nodded off to sleep. Quinter and Jennifer looked at each other.

"Did you ever get the feeling you had served your purpose?" Quinter said softly to Jennifer.

"You mean," she replied, "as in a bit superfluous?"

"Exactly. I'm happy you agreed to come."

LATER, WHEN QUINTER, Jennifer, and Bordman stepped onto the tarmac at Haverhill airport, the air was sweet, warm, and clear. They walked at a brisk pace to the terminal where they were met by yet another young man in a blue Nortex uniform.

"Good evening, Mr. Bordman." He picked up the two suitcases and the garment bag. "Right this way, sir."

Nodding pleasantly to Jennifer and Quinter, he said, "Good evening, my name is Felix."

The group followed Felix into and across the now-deserted terminal to a black limousine, which was parked in front of the entrance. Felix opened the door for his passengers, and when they were settled he got in the driver seat.

"I've been asked to take you to the company's guest quarters at the main office so you may freshen up and change, if you'd care to. I would then be pleased to take you to Mr. Johnson's residence to join the gathering."

"Excellent, Felix," replied Bordman.

At 9:00 pm, the limousine pulled up to the Nortex security gate. After nodding in recognition to Felix, the uniformed officer waived the vehicle through. Five minutes later, after Felix had followed the access road through a dense forest and then across an open moon-lit field, the lights of the limousine sequentially illuminated the four white columns of a two story brick Georgian structure. The porch lights shone brightly, displaying the red brick and the white windows.

Felix pulled the limo up to the door, got out of the vehicle, and opened each rear door. After popping the trunk, he handed small overnight bags to his guests, and then led them up the short walkway toward the door.

"You'll be quite comfortable here," Felix said to Quinter, "Your apartment is on the first floor to the right down the hallway, number two, the first door. We're pretty crowded so you and Ms. Millieux will share a two bedroom suite, if that is all right. Mr. Bordman, we've reserved apartment number three for you. Follow me please."

The group entered the building, walking into a large foyer, tastefully decorated in earth tones. Quinter, now in the lead, walked down the short corridor until he came to the first door on the right, noting the polished brass number 2. He opened the door and turned on the light. The living room was large, at least fifteen by eighteen feet, furnished with a brown leather sofa and two upholstered chairs arranged around a cherry coffee table.

Felix put the bags on a low rack next to the sofa and left to show Bordman his room. On his way out the door, he said, "I'll be back to pick you up in about forty minutes."

Quinter walked around the apartment. There were two bedrooms, separated by a bathroom, a kitchenette, and a breakfast nook.

"Do you mind if I take this one," he said, setting his suitcase on the king-sized bed in the blue bedroom.

"It's yours, Tom," Jennifer answered, walking toward the other bedroom.

"Tom, are you going to wear the suit?"

"I suppose so," he replied from the bedroom. "Just leave the bag on the sofa for me. I'm going to take a quick shower. Thanks."

The bathroom door closed as Jennifer returned to the living room. She unzipped the garment bag, laid Quinter's light gray suit over the backrest of the sofa. She carried her bag into her room, placed it on the bed, and removed a lavender sheath. She held the dress up in front of her while glancing into the full length mirror behind the bedroom door. The dress, one of her favorites, had white lace around the neckline which was cut just low enough to show the beginning curve of her breasts and more lace at the cuffs of the three-quarter length sleeves. The just-above-the-knee length was flattering, and the overall impression was interestingly revealing, but by no means an ostentatious presence.

"Your turn," Quinter shouted through the closed bathroom door. "We have about twenty minutes."

"I'll be ready," Jennifer replied. She entered the bathroom as the door closed from the other side, undressed, and took a quick hot shower. *This is all rather strange business,* she thought half-aloud, wrapping a towel around her upper body. *Everything seemed to be so well-planned.* She walked over to the full-length mirror and began to inspect herself closely.

Her mind drifted and she thought about the last Davis-James picnic, a time which seemed so long ago. She remembered the volleyball game, her sudden realization that Quinter was looking at her, and her spontaneous effort to attract him to her. She had wanted him to declare his interest in her.

Despite mutual danger, the course of their ensuing relationship had been defined by too many stolen moments and secret rendezvous, chosen to escape detection. The picnic had been two years ago, but she could still vividly recall the delicious touch of his warm hand on her bare waist as they had walked down the dusty road toward the lake below. She remembered . . .

"Jenny, we have ten minutes!" The sound of Quinter's voice shattered her mood bringing her back to reality with a jolt.

"*Damn*," she sighed to herself. "I know, Tom. Just a minute."

Quinter noted the hint of irritation in her voice.

"Jenny . . ." he replied, in similar tone, and allowing her name to trail off. He had been tightening the single overhand knot in the red and blue silk rep tie when he realized with dissatisfaction he had again misjudged the length. Knowing he should look his best for the evening, he untied the knot, and began to make the appropriate adjustment under the button down collar of the blue pin-point oxford shirt. He had just completed the task when he heard Felix's voice.

"We're ready, sir," Felix called.

"Right with you, Felix," said Quinter, turning his head from the mirror toward the bedroom door. "We'll meet you at the car. Jenny, will you please . . ." His thoughts became disorganized as he saw her closing the bedroom door behind her.

Lovely, he immediately thought. Her hair, filled with bronze highlights, was swept back, held in place by two lavender clips that matched her dress, pumps, and lipstick. *Lovely looking lady*. He felt a flash of desire which he could not completely conceal. Smiling sweetly, she replied "I'm ready, Tom."

Quinter took her arm, and they walked down the hallway of the guest residence toward the waiting limousine

4

MURDER IN HAVERHILL

ELIX OPENED THE DOOR TO the limo and the couple saw Bordman, drink in hand, seated in the jump seat.

"Care to join me?" he asked, raising a cut glass tumbler half full of ice and vodka. "My, Jennifer, don't you look lovely."

"Thank you," replied Jennifer in a formal tone, seating herself in the rear of the car. "I'll have a glass of white wine."

"In a moment, thanks," answered Quinter, sitting down next to Jennifer.

Felix started driving back toward the security gate. "It's a bit of a drive to Mr. Johnson's residence," he said matter-of-factly.

Bordman poured a glass of chardonnay for Jennifer.

"There will be twenty to twenty-five guests tonight," he began, "Among them Ralph Jones who has the responsibility for organizing the Energy Division which the Company has just formed. Quite a fellow. He joined us several months ago from British Petroleum where he oversaw the construction, and then operation of their entire Prudhoe Bay installation, including the pipeline. Also, there will be a couple of fellows from the State Department, one of them being young Tom Forbes, who was sort of a protégé of mine there, and an old friend of mine from the C.I.A. An interesting mix that should provide for an interesting evening."

As the limousine cruised toward Johnson's, Bordman engaged Jennifer in small talk. Quinter looked out the window just as the view changed from that of a densely wooded area to an open and expansive meadow. The western sky at the horizon was a soft velvety deep purple, but, at its darkest point it was still slightly lighter than the sky above it, even though the last rays of the sun had long since disappeared. The stars were many and brilliant, and the demarcation between star and universe was clear and distinct. Toward the south, Quinter could see billowy clouds and an occasional flash of heat lightning, and to the north, a thin sliver of moon carved a notch in the sky.

As he looked at the moon, Quinter's mind reconnected with an identical moon that he had watched, more than twenty five years earlier. He had been lying partially on the upper half of his dormitory cot in Webster, with his forearms resting on the window sill, and his chin on his overlapping hands, looking through one eye at that same sliver of moon as it rose above Amen hall to his right.

QUINTER LIFTED HIS head to free his left hand, and, touching the bandage across his right eye gingerly, he moved his fingers outward, pressing the lengths of adhesive tape against his forehead and temple. His senses were clear now, but a dull throb synchronized to his slow heartbeat still ached deep in his brain. He had just returned to Webster after his last class at the Academy Building, and he was tired. His mind, scrolling backwards, recalled the events of Saturday.

It wasn't until he woke up in the Lamont infirmary that Quinter felt the first sharp excruciating pain, and then he remembered the disorientation, the red-blackness, and, finally, the big Andover fullback coming straight at him inside Exeter's five yard line. There was no one else left to stop this lumbering behemoth.

Despite his fear, Quinter had crashed into the monster and brought him down at the two yard line, just as the game-ending whistle blew. He never saw the fullback's knee smash into the orbit of his right eye, nor heard the roar of the crowd exulting in Exeter's one point margin of victory.

His first memory was being assisted from the field, each arm supported by a loyal teammate. The short trip on the stretcher, and the longer drive to the Lamont infirmary in the ambulance, were a confusing semi-conscious blur, and it was several hours before pain's sharp sword slashed through this kindly veil. Quinter raised his head and again smoothed the tape, this time against his cheek. The dull ache caused him to re-focus on the slender moon.

He remembered his father's firm words of principle, spoken in front of an enormous pile of brick Quinter had committed to stack: "A task once undertaken must be completed in a workman-like manner." Only after he had begun the job did he realize that the secret lies in making the correct initial decision: either undertake the task or let it pass. And he had worked long and hard that afternoon to earn his three dollars.

"Tom," said Jennifer, nudging him gently in the ribs to get his attention, "Dave is asking you if you have changed your mind about that drink."

"Sure," replied Quinter, returning his attention to the interior of the limousine. "Scotch on the rocks."

The car moved on into the night. After a few minutes, Felix slowed and turned right into a driveway, continued a hundred yards, and stopped at a heavy iron gate. An armed security guard came out from a small guard station, and, recognizing Felix flipped the gate switch to open.

"Good evening, Felix," he said, "most of the guests have already arrived, and Mr. Johnson is waiting for you."

"Thanks," said Felix, as he started up the driveway.

After they'd gone about a third of a mile, Jennifer caught sight of the residence, which was located up on a knoll to the left. Flood lights illuminated the six imposing white fluted pillars that were evenly spaced across the front of the building. The colonial architecture was similar to that of the main guest quarters they had just left.

Preceded by Bordman and followed by Felix, Quinter and Jennifer walked up the flagstone steps. They were met at the front door by a gentleman's gentleman dressed in black tie.

"Good evening," he said, in a formal manner. "This way, please."

"It is a good evening, Jamison," replied Bordman. "And it's good to see you again."

"Sir," acknowledged Jamison.

As he followed the others into the center hall, Quinter caught a flash of summer lightening, and then, a few moments later, he heard the low rumble of distant thunder.

The red oak hardwood floor of the center hall was covered almost entirely by a large oriental rug. An impressive staircase began at the right side, leading to a landing enclosed on two sides by windows. Six foot palms graced either side of the entrance. Adjacent to the stairs stood an enormous grandfather clock with intricate wood patterns, spires, and a multi-colored face of inlaid metals. Opposite the clock was a small table with a large vertical mirror. The dining room was located off the center hall to the right, and was dominated by a long mahogany table with seven Early

American chairs placed along each side, another at the head, and one at the foot.

The melodic sounds of piano jazz softly filled the large living room. A number of people were standing, talking in groups of threes and fours. Others were seated on various sofas and chairs.

As Jamison escorted Quinter, Jennifer, and Bordman into the room, a man wearing a camel hair jacket and brown slacks rose from his chair at the far end of the room, and began threading his way through the assembled guests. He approached the trio, and, with a friendly smile, extended his hand to Bordman.

"Hello, David, right on schedule as always."

"Thanks Duane," replied Bordman, "I'd like you to meet Jennifer Millieux and an old friend of mine, Tom Quinter."

"Pleasure to meet you," said Johnson smoothly, extending his hand to each of them in turn.

"Duane Johnson. I trust you had a pleasant journey and are not too fatigued to enjoy yourselves for the remainder of the evening."

"You made it an easy trip, for which we thank you," said Quinter picking up the politesse of the moment, sensing that Johnson was a man of enormous political skills.

"Happy to oblige. Glad you could come," replied Johnson. "Come, allow me to introduce you to my wife and the others."

Mathilde 'Matty' Johnson turned out to be a stout woman in her mid-fifties. While she had an easy and open manner, she moved in small, choppy steps, possessing little of the savoir-faire that obviously was of the essence of her husband. Jennifer seemed to like her instantly, a connection reciprocated as the two women fell into a comfortable conversation.

Johnson introduced Quinter to Butler, the company's new security chief, and Tester, the public information officer, before excusing himself to re-engage in a conversation with his son, which quickly became intense.

"I understand you are going to assist us in scouting around and obtaining some Spanish real estate," said Butler, matter-of-factly.

"That's the plan," said Quinter.

"Spain is a fascinating and beautiful country," continued Butler, sizing up Quinter. "Don't you think so, Korny?"

"Absolutely," responded Tester, "and the señoritas, *Oh là là*. Better than American women."

"Korny and I spent two weeks there last month, mostly in Madrid. Have you ever been to Spain, Mr. Quinter?"

"A number of times. The southern part primarily. No business, just vacation."

"You must know all about the Spanish ladies, huh Thomas? Bet you've even bedded a few." injected Tester, crudely.

"The Costa del Sol has to be one of the most beautiful coasts in the world," Quinter replied, ignoring Tester's comment. Then, unable to resist, he added, "Korny. That's with a 'C', isn't it?"

As Butler chuckled softly, Tester considered Quinter's comment for a moment and then, deciding that he did not like the tone, answered edgily, "Whatever you like, my man. Whatever you like. Well, it's getting a little close in here. I think I'll go chat with Ralph Jones over there."

"That's a good idea," replied Quinter smiling, and meeting Tester's glaring eyes. Tester did not respond, but turned and left the group as Johnson returned, bringing with him a tall, older gentleman immaculately dressed in a double-breasted blue suit, and a yellow tie that had light-blue horses jumping fences. His elegant, carefully-waxed white handlebar moustache was parallel to the horizon and his hair, which was also white, was combed back revealing a high forehead. He had an engaging full smile.

"Tom, I would like you to meet Sir Bertram Reynolds," said Johnson.

"Pleased to make your acquaintance, Sir Bertram," said Quinter, extending his hand.

"Pleasure is mine, my good sir. Understand you and the young lady will be joining us when we depart day after the morrow."

"Is that the plan?" responded Quinter, making no effort to conceal his surprise at learning the proximity of the departure.

A thunderclap startled the group as the first raindrops of the summer storm fell against the windows that faced the driveway.

"Oh yes, old chap. All in the schedule. Well, Duane, I am off. I must say that it has been absolutely delightful. I particularly enjoyed the wonderfully inventive music. So lively. But it's nearing 11:00, and I have several matters to attend to before our meeting in the morning. Would you mind having Jamison fetch my car? I do so love to drive that car-particularly in the rain. Great response, wonderful balance. Fantastic traction."

"Certainly," replied Johnson. "Come. I'll walk you to the door." Sir Bertram said his good-byes and then he and Johnson, arm in arm, walked toward the front door.

"Interesting man," said Butler, breaking the silence which had fallen after another roll of thunder. "I'm told he was a friend of Franco's, and became involved in refurbishing the Spanish Navy after World War II. A connoisseur of Arabic architecture as well, if I'm not mistaken. Don't get him started talking about the Alhambra unless you have an hour or so."

"I'll bear that in mind," said Quinter smiling, "but I must admit it is one of the most impressive places I've ever visited."

Just then, Jennifer and Mrs. Johnson approached the three men. "Mind if we join you?" Matty asked pleasantly.

The wind was now beginning to drive the rain drops against the windows, and the sporadic ping of hailstones sounded, intermingled with flashes of lightening and accompanying thunder.

"Our pleasure. Looks like we're in for a little weather," remarked Quinter.

"It'll pass quickly," promised Matty. "And you two should take advantage of the dance floor," she continued, looking first at Quinter and then Jennifer, while gesturing toward an area in the far corner of the room where several couples were dancing.

"A great idea," said Quinter, "don't you think so, Jenny?" he said as he grasped her hand.

"Sure," she replied, and they moved toward the dance floor.

As Quinter and Jennifer reached the dancing area, the jazz trio began the first bars of "Embraceable You".

"You up for going to Spain the day after tomorrow?" said Quinter as he folded Jennifer into his arms, noticing how good she felt.

"Matty told me that was 'on the schedule'," she answered. "A bit abrupt, don't you think?"

"Bordman never did give me a date. I learned it for the first time when Sir Bertram mentioned it a few moments ago. By the way, I didn't bring much in the way of clothes," continued Quinter.

"Me neither. Maybe we could do some shopping tomorrow," answered Jennifer.

"According to Bordman, we have a meeting with Johnson at ten, but I think we could pick up some things in the early afternoon," said Quinter. "If everyone knew the departure was tomorrow, someone should have let us know. Also, I told my old law school roommate, Jeff Downing, we would try to drive out and spend some time with him and Martha in Gloucester later in the afternoon. I'd like to do that if at all possible."

Jennifer nodded, remembering the water color painting of the Maine seascape in Quinter's apartment.

"What do you think of this business? What about the people?" Quinter continued, changing the subject.

"Not exactly what I expected," she began, "but then I hadn't given them much thought. I like Matty, but I am uncomfortable with her husband. Tester's superficially handsome with the blond hair and those baby blues, but also an ass—and maybe dangerous. Butler is quietly efficient and I think trustworthy. I did meet Johnson's son. He's over there, the young man with glasses, talking to the lady in green. Seems a little edgy, almost scared. By the way, did you have a chance to meet Ralph Jones?"

"Not yet," Quinter replied, pausing to reflect on Jennifer's first impressions, "but you certainly summed up my feelings about the others."

"Well, you won't like Jones," she continued, "He's the most evasive person I've met in a long time. Never looks you in the eye. He's the one in the gray blazer and white slacks talking to Johnson."

"I'm sure I'll have the opportunity to meet him soon," replied Quinter, his voice trailing off as he brought her closer to him. She touched his cheek with hers and he became aware of her breasts against his chest. He thought he heard a slight catch in her breath.

"You feel so good, Jenny," he whispered in her ear.

"Mmmmmm," she murmured, allowing herself to be caught up in the moment. A brilliant flash and loud crack of thunder startled her, causing her to flinch.

"That was pretty close," said Quinter, holding her tightly.

Instead of replying, Jennifer laid her head on his shoulder.

They danced for several minutes in silence before a large buffet against the far wall caught Quinter's attention. Realizing he was hungry and remembering they'd had only a light snack on the plane, Quinter danced Jennifer toward the buffet.

The offering was spectacular. A variety of fish and crustaceans and a wide selection of meats and fowl were tastefully presented on the finest Lenox china. Ornate silver platters were piled high with raw and cooked vegetables—each surrounded by a number of sauces in little blue china bowls with gold rims. A separate table held a vast selection of desserts, pies, tortes, fresh fruit, and cakes. As Quinter was selecting various delicacies, he gradually became aware of an angular young man looking at him in a friendly manner from the other side of the buffet.

"An interesting spread," he began, "I'm Tom Forbes, and this is my friend, Janet Jacobson."

"Tom Quinter and this is *my* friend, Jennifer Millieux."

"You arrived just in time for one of our notorious Massachusetts storms."

"Yes," replied Quinter. "We arrived earlier this evening. Doesn't this food look amazing?"

"Why don't you and Jennifer join us? We're sitting at the small table across from the piano," said Forbes gesturing toward an area near the musicians.

"Oh, please do," encouraged Janet.

Quinter looked toward Jennifer who nodded and said, "Sure."

The two couples completed their selections and moved across the room toward the table which Janet had secured with her purse. The conversation soon turned to work.

Forbes said he was in the Middle Eastern section of the State Department in an intermediate level capacity, a position he had held for about eighteen months. His present project was to assemble as much information as possible about the demographics of the Iranian population, and then to begin a reclassification based upon various political interests.

"Most Americans," he began, "think the Iranian political structure is monolithic under the Ayatollah, but in reality there are numerous diverse groups which all interact in some measure with the religious apparatus."

"I had always imagined the Iranian State controlled everything and everyone, using the Muslim faith as an instrument," said Jennifer.

"They do, to be sure," continued Forbes," but take, for example, the oil industry. The business is actually operated by technocrats and businessmen who are always looking for private methods to increase production and sales. The religious state, of course, always has the final say, but the oil interests are very much encouraged to open new channels for trade—when they have oil to trade.

"But don't they *always* have oil to trade?" interrupted Jennifer.

"You'd think so, wouldn't you, but it seems that the Iraqis are forever bombing the facilities. The Iranian Government says that when oil production and sale reach 35% of the capacity that was routine under the Shah it's been a good month."

"I suppose I never will understand that situation," added Janet. "The Tigress and Euphrates rivers are thought by some to have been one of the earliest birthplaces of the human race, and yet they are still killing one another with abandon. Kind of ironic."

"It is difficult to comprehend," commented Quinter, "but, for sure, there's going to be one hell of a fight before long.

And if that happens, as things stand now, Saddam would give them a thrashing—unless the Iranians got their hands on some first-class equipment. But, of course the Iraqis will go to any extreme to prevent that from happening."

After a brief internal debate, Quinter suddenly said, "I don't mean to be rude, but why are you here tonight, Tom?"

Forbes smiled. "Actually, that's a good question. I believe Nortex thinks I might be able to shed some light on who in the Middle East would be 'parties of interest' as far as their Spanish venture is concerned." And then, with a small laugh, he added, "They must think I'm much higher up in the power structure at State. I believe I owe my presence here tonight to Dave Bordman. He and I worked on a number of projects together in his last couple of years before he left for the private sector."

"Thanks, Tom," said Quinter. "I have a tendency to be direct, at times perhaps too direct. I like to think of it as a Midwestern virtue, but not everyone agrees."

"Now, please excuse me for a moment," said Quinter. He got up and began heading in the direction of the hallway restroom.

As he approached the doorway to the center hall, Quinter felt a rush of wind. Looking to his right, he saw two deputy sheriffs standing in the foyer, their rain gear dripping, the half-opened front door held against the wind by the heel of one of the deputy's boots. In front, stood Johnson and the butler, Jamison.

Drawn by the obvious drama, Quinter joined the group just as Johnson exclaimed, "My God! Sir Bertram's dead? That's not possible! He just left here, not forty-five minutes ago."

"Yes, sir," replied one of the officers, "The Bentley went off the road and crashed through the brush into Silver creek, about five miles from here.

"Also, sir . . . he was shot—at close range."

The color drained from Johnson's face.

"Those Bastards!" he said.

"Sir?" questioned the officer.

"Anything I can do?" asked Johnson.

"No, sir, we'll handle the business from here. But we did think that you should know right away. We'll be going now, sir. Nasty night for this kind of business. G'night." The officers left, closing the door behind them.

Noticing Quinter, Johnson asked, "You heard what happened?"

"I did," Tom replied.

T HERE WAS LITTLE conversation in the limo during the return trip to the Nortex guest quarters. Felix let his passengers off at the front door and Bordman, Jennifer, and Quinter walked down the first floor corridor together. "The meeting will go forward at 10:00 tomorrow. I'll pick you up at 9:00 o'clock for breakfast," Bordman said, and he left the couple at the door to apartment 2, not waiting for a reply.

As Quinter and Jennifer entered the apartment, Jenifer said, "I'm exhausted."

"I know. Jesus, what a turn of events. I'll see you in the morning, Jenny. But, first, I think I should check this place out."

He walked to the windows in Jennifer's bedroom, checking the locks and evaluating the security. Satisfied, he surveyed the remaining windows in the apartment, and then closed the dead bolt, engaging the locking chain.

"Good night, Jenny, we'll talk more tomorrow," and he closed the bedroom door.

He retrieved the small suitcase from the closet, and, removed the shoulder holster and Mauser. He unsnapped one of the loaded magazine pockets, and removing the cool metal, shoved it home in the butt of the Mauser. He placed the weapon on the small night table next to the bed and hung the holster over the maple bed post. He stripped and lay down under the sheet, wondering softly aloud, *"'Those Bastards', huh? That's a funny choice of words."* His thoughts drifted until sleep came.

5

QUINTER GETS A RAISE

THE FIRST RAYS OF SUN filtering through the window fell on Quinter's left cheek, warming it slightly. He sat up in the bed, noting with satisfaction that he was refreshed. He looked at his watch. It was 20 minutes after 6:00. Wrapping a towel around his middle, he walked into the bathroom and started the shower.

The hot water felt therapeutic as it flooded over his head. Well, he thought, this *was* going to be an adventure. In fact, it had already been an adventure—perhaps too much of an adventure. He had a nagging instinct he was being carried along by larger, unknown forces. *"Pawn to King four,"* he murmured to himself, *"the best opening move in chess."* He had adopted this original expression from his stepfather who liked to use it whenever the circumstances seemed to call for a proven approach.

He finished showering and shaving quickly, uttering a soft expletive as he nicked the right side of his jaw under the chin. He walked into the bedroom and took a pair of slacks and a shirt from the closet, selected a charcoal grey crew neck sweater from the bureau drawer, pulled it over his shirt, and finished dressing. He returned to the living room, sat at the desk for a brief moment to scribble a note for Jennifer, propped the note up on the seat against the back of a chair he had placed by the apartment door, and left .

A clock in the distance was striking 7:00 as Quinter walked out the front door of the guest quarters. The sun was well up and the air crystal clear and cool. His attention was caught by the eight-foot high chain-link fence at a distance of about one third of a mile directly in front of and paralleling the building. Even from where he was, Quinter could see the fence was topped with V-shape strands of barbed razor wire that extended upward for another two feet.

To his left, the fence led down about two miles to the security gate house. To his right, it continued for about a mile before turning to the right, up and over a hill behind him, and disappeared from sight. Around the guest quarters for a hundred yards in every direction was a well-kept lawn dotted by numerous flower gardens and large maple trees which extended beyond the lawn and throughout the meadow.

When Quinter walked around the rear of the guest quarters, he noticed a swimming pool. *If I had seen it earlier, I'd have gone for a morning dip*, he thought. Off in the distance to the right of the hill behind the guest quarters, he saw eight to ten two and three story buildings. The building in the center was taller than the rest and had a large white dome, topped with what appeared to be a tinted glass roof.

He began walking up the hill to get a better vantage point. Cresting the hill, he noticed a two to three acre compound in the valley below, surrounded by a fence. A green and brown mottled canvas covered the lower portion of the fence, and the V-shaped razor wire at the top was unmistakable.

54

Three huge hangers, painted in camouflage, blended into the surroundings.

Quinter walked down the grassy slope which was still wet with the early morning dew, and in a few minutes reached the canvas-covered fence, which now obscured all but the roofs of the low hangers. Lengths of canvas 50 feet long by eight feet high were periodically attached to the chain link fence by short pieces of twisted wire.

He followed the fence until he came to a gap in the barrier, and then, pausing, he looked through the bare chain links to the hangers beyond. In front of the nearest hanger, parked at a distance of about 30 yards, were four M-1 A-1 tanks, the muzzles of their turret guns still wrapped in a dark brown protective material. The fresh paint was the color of sand, even at the point where the exhaust stack left the engine compartment. These war machines were brand new.

Seeing no activity, and feeling uncomfortable, Quinter turned away from the fence and began walking back up the hill. Reaching the crest, he heard the barking of dogs coming from the security gate in the distance. An amplified crackling voice split the early morning quiet.

"Please remain where you are, sir. You are in a restricted area. We are sending someone to get you. I repeat. Please remain where you are and proceed no further."

Startled, Quinter looked in the direction from which the sound had come. On a large maple off to his left, he saw a television camera mounted on a platform next to a loudspeaker. At the same moment, he observed a military jeep leaving the security gate.

Quinter leaned against a large rock, watching the progress of the jeep as it came toward him. The vehicle stopped on the dirt road, and two Nortex security officers got out and began walking uphill toward him. The short leather straps restraining their forty-five caliber pistols were unsnapped. He waited at the rock as the officers approached.

"A bit touchy, aren't you?" said Quinter not very pleasantly.

"Sorry, Sir. But you are in an unauthorized area. We'll need to take you back to the guest quarters."

"You certainly don't mark your unauthorized areas." continued Quinter flatly.

"Sorry, Sir, but we'll have to take you back now. Mr. Quinter, isn't it?"

"Correct," snapped Quinter, as he walked toward the jeep, followed by the officers. When he passed in front of the jeep, he continued across the road and down the hill toward the guest residence.

"I think I'll walk back from here," said Quinter over his shoulder in the direction of the two security guards who were now standing with their hands on their hips.

"Alright," replied the taller of the guards as Quinter walked off toward the swimming pool, "but please proceed directly to your quarters."

Quinter heard the motor rev. As he glanced over his shoulder, the jeep made a U-turn and came to a stop on the road facing in the opposite direction. He continued walking toward the guest quarters, and as he reached the cut grass lawn, he heard the engine rev again. Taking a second look without breaking stride, he saw the jeep begin the return trek to the security gate.

Quinter walked into the guest quarters, down the hall, and opened the door of apartment number two. Jennifer was seated at the table in the breakfast nook taking a sip from her coffee cup.

"Care for some, Tom? Bordman won't be here for half an hour. How was your walk?"

"Interesting," said Quinter and he told her about his observations and the encounter with Nortex security.

Jennifer listened intently, and then said, "It sounds like they were a little touchy, but Tom, Nortex *is* a government military contractor. I would think they must be careful especially when it comes to people they don't know."

"I guess you're right, but the whole incident galls me. And the tank business doesn't make any sense. Nortex stopped making and selling tanks about a year ago and sold the business to General Dynamics. Now they're supposed to be missile and arms manufacturers solely. You know, Jenny, you don't need to go ahead with this. Some pretty rough people are involved, and we don't know what we're in for."

"I'm a guy with a military background who has bounced around a bit and wants some adventure—and I think I'll ask them for more money for the additional trouble—but there could be real danger. I don't know that you really want to run the risk. Also, I would have a hard time forgiving myself if anything happened to you."

"Thomas Quinter, I've already thought about this and decided that I want to be part of whatever is going on. You are assuming, of course, that any danger is more personal to us than we know. So, I'm in, and the matter is settled."

Quinter was surprised by the firmness in her voice.

"Well, Jenny, I was just . . ."

Jennifer had gotten up and walked over to where Quinter was sitting at the table. She placed her hand on his shoulder and looked down at him.

"I know, Tom, and I appreciate your concern, but I also need to make my own decisions. And I have made my decision. I am here and no matter what happens, I'm in it for the long haul."

"Pawn to King four . . ." muttered Quinter, while thinking, *This woman has some steel in her.*

"What, Tom?"

"Nothing," he replied.

At 10 minutes before 9:00, Jennifer answered Bordman's knock at the door.

"I'm a little early, but good morning anyway." he said looking at Quinter with a slight smile. "I hear you've been up for a while. No reason not to get the day under way. Felix will be here soon."

"I ran into some of your security people during my walk this morning. A bit sensitive, I thought," countered Quinter.

"Don't be offended, Tom. The security folks were just doing their job. Military types, you know."

"Well, I'm not terribly offended and I do have some knowledge of these matters. But tell me, Dave, what's in the compound?"

"I understand there are several pretty sophisticated guidance system prototypes, some high speed pumps and other equipment for the new Energy division, and the first shipment of materiel for the Spanish deal. Who knows what else," answered Bordman. "But, let's go. Felix will be waiting, not to mention the rest of our breakfast companions. You'll learn more later, as needed."

Felix indeed was waiting.

"Good morning," he said. "Breakfast will be at the Rotunda."

Felix drove the limousine down the paved road to the security gate, and then turned left toward the buildings Quinter had seen earlier. As they approached them, Quinter counted ten structures. Some buildings had two stories, but there were more with three. In the middle of the complex was a large five-story structure with a glass-roofed dome which Quinter had seen earlier. The remainder of the buildings, all Georgian in architecture, were set around the Rotunda.

"This is hard to believe," remarked Jennifer looking at the meticulously manicured lawns, unbroken, except by the many flower gardens and the strips of white concrete sidewalk that led from building to building. "This is a little city out here in the middle of nowhere."

"Just what we call it, ma'am," replied Felix. "Little City is the international headquarters of the Nortex Corporation. Business offices are located in the Rotunda and the three buildings on your left. The remaining buildings are for research and development."

Steady streams of people were moving between the buildings, many carrying papers, blueprints, or briefcases. Occasionally an officer dressed in the uniform of one of the armed services would appear, sometimes accompanied by an attaché or liaison officer. Quinter's overall impression was one of method and orderliness.

The limo passed a large asphalt parking lot that was filled to near-capacity, and turned into the Rotunda driveway, stopping underneath the portecochere. Two armed security guards, one on either side of the double doors, came to attention as the trio entered the Rotunda.

Inside, the entrance opened onto a large circular room ringed by massive white marble columns. The core of the structure extended the full five floors to the blue-tinted convex glass ceiling of the dome which was separated into panels by white lattice work. A balcony of twisted red wrought iron was located at each floor level between the columns, and a gold Nortex coat of arms was displayed in the center of each section. Beyond each balcony, hallways led away from the central position like spokes in a wheel.

Quinter and Jennifer followed Bordman to the elevator bank and waited amidst a gathering crowd. When the elevator arrived, Bordman signaled for the fifth floor, and in no time, the three were looking down at the blue and white tile floor and the bustle of the people below.

"I'm impressed," said Jennifer breaking the silence.

"A lot happens here," said Bordman, starting down one of the hallways as the clock in the dome began striking nine in deep melodic tones. He paused for an instant before a large paneled set of double mahogany doors, knocked softly two times, and pushed one of the doors open.

Duane Johnson was sitting behind an immense tabletop desk at the far end of the room. In front of him were four comfortable overstuffed tan leather chairs, and behind him double French doors and a balcony that overlooked the grounds. To his right sat his son Joel and to his left, Ralph Jones, President of Energia, the new Nortex energy division.

"Good morning, David," said Johnson in a calm yet slightly intense manner. "Right on time, as usual."

"Good morning, Duane," said Bordman who then greeted Johnson's son and Jones. After the pleasantries, Johnson suggested the group adjourn for breakfast to a small adjoining room.

"Best breakfast in town," he said smiling, "and no charge."

The six people seated themselves at a glass-topped table. Johnson, at the head of the table, touched a button on the wall to his left, and immediately two waitresses appeared. In no time, the table was filled with silver platters brimming with steaming individual omelets, muffins, fruit, French toast, rolls, and various meats.

"I have some information concerning the death of Sir Bertram," Johnson began. "The Boston police apprehended two suspects, both Iraqi, at Logan airport. The men had tried to return a damaged rental car without declaring an accident, and the attendant called the police. When the police began to question the pair, they tried to run, but were caught. I've been told the rental vehicle had silver paint scrape markings. The lab analysis will confirm whether or not the paint is identical to that of Sir Bertram's Bentley, but they believe a match is likely. No weapon has been located."

"What do you make of the incident?" asked Quinter.

"Well," said Johnson, his eyes narrowing, "several possibilities are being investigated. First, I understand David has mentioned to you, a number of people do not want Spain to engage in the military build-up the United States and NATO believe to be so critical at this time. It seems they can't separate the politics between that and the present Iran-Iraq war.

"But it's a big jump," he continued, in what Quinter thought was a less confident tone, "from protestors to assassins. So that's an X-factor, an unknown, at least for now."

"In addition, there are substantial Spanish political groups that believe Spain's overall national interest does not coincide with membership in NATO. These groups want Spain to select a more neutral course between the alliance and the Warsaw Pact, a more non-aligned position, if you will. For years, the Soviets have been trying to cause dissatisfaction with NATO in an effort to undermine the European balance of power, and our Spanish deal has become something of a test of international will. If the military build-up is not undertaken, and Spain's formal ties with NATO are weakened, it will set an extremely bad precedent. Such a course of action could well lead to reduced participation by others in the organization, if not outright defection."

Johnson paused for a moment, and then went on. "It was well known that Sir Bertram was one of the spokesmen for the U.S. NATO position, and he had great influence with many leading members of the Spanish Government. His death will certainly be a blow to securing and maintaining speedy approval from the Spaniards. We do believe, however, that this approval can still be secured." Johnson took a sip of coffee.

"On the other hand, his death might be a far more personal proposition. Sir Bertram's friendship with Franco over the years brought him great access, but also made him many enemies since he was associated with a number of unpopular acts and policies. For example, after World War II when Sir Bertram was given the task of rebuilding the Spanish Navy, a cadre of high-ranking officers from the other Spanish services openly opposed Franco's decision and actively tried to reverse it. Franco executed six of them and imprisoned several others.

"It was widely believed at the time that Sir Bertram suggested this 'solution' to Franco. There are other examples, but I think you get the gist."

The waitresses had returned to clear the breakfast dishes. Johnson pushed himself away from the table and the others followed him back to the office. The group sat around a coffee table on a sofa and the several chairs in front of Johnson's desk. From his position on the sofa next to Jennifer, Quinter, looking through the French doors leading to the balcony, could see several large puffy white clouds beginning to form at the horizon across the meadow and behind the farthest maples.

As Johnson walked across the room to open the balcony doors, Quinter looked at Jones, seated to his right. Jones was slender of build and just short of six feet tall. Not a powerful man, Quinter thought to himself, but noted that Jones's wiry physique probably was indicative of a good deal of stamina.

"Do you live nearby?" Quinter asked him, in a preliminary effort to be polite while taking the measure of the man.

"The Company was good enough to provide me a house not too far from Mr. Johnson's," answered Jones, scarcely looking up from his hands, the fingers of which he had intertwined in his lap.

"What do you do here, Ralph?" pressed Quinter.

Johnson, who by this time had returned to the group and seated himself across from Quinter between his son and Jones, interjected, "Ralph is going to make our new division, Energia, a most profitable venture, isn't that true, Ralph."

"You can count on it, Mr. Johnson," Jones replied.

"I tell you these things," Johnson continued as though there had been no interruption, "since it occurred to me, Thomas, that the task we asked you to undertake may entail more difficulty than you originally contemplated, not to mention any concerns which Miss Millieux may have. I do wish to reiterate, however, that it is important to the company to act through an agent who has no known company affiliation—particularly in view of recent events.

"As David has advised you, and now that the situation is even more complex, we have determined that we need access to a secure house for meeting and lodging purposes. In addition, we will need another area that is a little more remote, with perhaps some land, which we could use as a transfer station for our people and our goods. As I feel an obligation for the safety of my employees, I mean to do all I can to protect them during the course of this operation.

"David tells me that you are a man of some resources and know the area. More importantly, though, I've heard that if you could be persuaded to accept the job, you would do so with unquestioned loyalty. Finally, of course, it has occurred to me that you and Miss Millieux present us with a perfect cover. What do you say? Are you still in?"

Quinter had been listening intently. Johnson's explanation seemed to make sense, and, looked at objectively, the element of personal danger to him and to Jennifer, despite the event in his Cleveland office, seemed remote. So did the possibility of there being any connection between it and his new venture—especially when viewed from the comfort of Nortex's luxurious corporate headquarters in faraway Massachusetts.

"I am inclined to go forward with the job," said Quinter in a thoughtful tone, "but this business with Sir Bertram is troubling, as is the apparent interest of the Iraqis. These present new elements of risk. My father always believed the reward should be commensurate with the risk, and I tend to agree with him."

Quinter, as he often did in trial, had allowed his voice to trail off gradually and become replaced by the faintest of smiles.

Johnson pressed on. "What would you think is a 'commensurate reward,'" he asked, almost innocently.

Quinter, who understood it was always better to be the recipient of an offer, continued the verbal fencing.

"Well, Duane, I would think you are better-positioned to assess the risk than I."

"Tom, I think that under the circumstances three thousand dollars a day plus expenses ought to cover all of the various contingencies."

Quinter appeared to contemplate the offer for a moment, and, completely suppressing his pleasant shock at the amount, replied, "Agreed." The two men shook hands.

"David will work out the details with you," said Johnson as he stood up. "By the way, my son Joel will be replacing Sir Bertram as the Company's chief spokesman and coordinator." Quinter looked at Joel who smiled nervously in return. "He'll do well. Harvard graduate, you know," continued Johnson as he escorted Quinter, Jennifer, and Bordman to the door.

"Good-bye. And have an enjoyable and successful trip," said Johnson, closing the doors behind him.

As the trio headed toward the elevator, Bordman picked up the conversation where Johnson had stopped.

"Not much to work out in the way of details," he said. "We will be leaving for Madrid tomorrow night at 8:00 o'clock, with a stop in Lisbon to drop Jones to inspect our two new tankers."

"Fine," answered Quinter, "Jenny and I have some shopping to do. Any chance of a car?"

"I would think so," said Bordman. "Incidentally," he continued, "we'll need a passport picture for Jennifer delivered to the officer at the security gate by 6:00 o'clock. I understand that yours is in order. And I'm sure you have a license for the pistol."

"I'm all set on both counts," replied Quinter in measured tones as the significance of Bordman's comment became clear to him. "You folks don't leave much to chance, do you, Dave?" he said pushing the elevator call button.

"As little as we can," answered Bordman. "I'm going to work in my office for a while. Felix will take you wherever you want."

"I think that Jenny and I will return to the guest quarters for a bit, and when you send the car, we'll go into Haverhill. I did tell my law school roommate that, if at all possible, I would drive over to Gloucester and visit him this evening, so perhaps we can meet for lunch tomorrow."

"Fine," said Bordman as the elevator door opened.

Felix was waiting as Quinter and Jennifer walked out the front door of the Rotunda, past the security guards. Quinter noted there was no salute. After holding the car door, Felix returned to the driver's seat and began driving toward the guest quarters. As he neared the security gate, the telephone buzzed.

"Yes sir," he answered, "I will, sir," and he replaced the receiver in the cradle. "The car will be delivered to you by eleven o'clock, Mr. Quinter."

"Thanks, Felix," replied Quinter as the limousine approached its destination.

6

'LOBSTA' WITH THE DOWNINGS

JENNIFER SAT AT THE DRESSING table in front of the mirror brushing her hair. She glanced out the window at the long shadows cast by the late afternoon sun. The day had passed swiftly, she thought, looking at the mirrored reflection of the skirts, blouses, sweaters and other purchases she had made earlier, basically everything she would need for the trip to Spain.

Not a bad haul, courtesy of Nortex, she thought, smiling to herself as she recalled the boyish expression on Quinter's face when she modeled various outfits, purposefully striking provocative poses in front of the three-sided mirror while Quinter looked on, his discomfort increasingly apparent. She had enjoyed every moment of her deliberate effort to tease him, and particularly so when she saw him blush.

Jennifer had never understood why Tom had stopped seeing her after his separation from Natalie. But unquestionably,

Jennifer's romantic relationship with him began to deteriorate, and she could not get him to discuss it. For a while she had been crestfallen, thinking that perhaps once the fruit was no longer forbidden, he had found it no longer desirable.

She was aware Quinter had given serious consideration to leaving Davis-James for several months before he resigned, that he'd become disaffected with the long hours, and had developed a genuine disdain for the petty personal politics that was so much a part of the fabric of the institution. The artificiality of the incessant dinner parties with clients, and the power lunches with partners jockeying for position in the firm and work assignment, had begun to seem unimportant on the relative scale by which he was now measuring his life.

Then too, as Tom had told her, there was the strange, tense conversation with Mr. Davis in the fall of 1985 when Davis had stopped by Quinter's office after lunch.

"Tom, how long have we been partners, now? Nine or ten years?" Davis had begun as he seated himself stiffly on the sofa adjacent to Quinter's desk.

"Sounds right to me, Nate," he had answered guardedly, knowing Davis's custom was not to go to other lawyers' offices for light conversation.

"Well, let me be frank, Tom. You have had a brilliant record here at the firm. Lost only three cases, and if I recall correctly, one of those could not legitimately be considered a loss. But Tom, I have a nagging feeling you are not attached, or should I say, committed to the firm. Now Tom, I don't expect all partners to agree 100% with the direction of the firm at any moment, but loyalty to the firm and its interests are important qualities, and, of course, Natalie's concerned."

"I'm not quite sure I follow you, Nate." Quinter replied coolly, while thinking *Damn, she's been complaining to her father again.*

"I have this vague thought, Tom, that you are not happy . . . that you may have interests which are distracting you from attaining life's real goals. And you might want to listen a little more to what Natalie wants. As I said, Tom, commitment is an important quality."

"I suppose everyone questions direction from time to time," Quinter replied.

"Yes, Tom," Davis had answered while rising from the sofa and heading toward the door, "and perhaps this is your time to reconsider your direction. Nothing urgent, but I wouldn't let the process drag on too long."

As he left Quinter's office, Mr. Davis said, "Give my love to Natalie."

In the late fall of 1986, one month after Quinter's divorce from Natalie was final, Quinter told Jennifer he was planning to leave Davis-James at the end of the year to open his own office. He asked her to come with him and manage the new undertaking. In spite of the cut in pay, she accepted.

After Quinter opened "THOMAS M. QUINTER and ASSOCIATES" on January 1, and for the first few months of 1987, they had been constant companions in business and love. But since then, and for no reason Jennifer could discover, Quinter's ardor had cooled, leaving her confused and frustrated. Some of her confusion arose because she could not understand what was holding him back, now that they were both free to follow their hearts.

Occasionally she wondered if the unworkable romantic triangle had simply been a hurtful game. Yet, he had never given her any reason to believe that he was anything but sincere in his feelings for her. She attributed some of the problem to Quinter's frustration with his inability to bring as many clients to Quinter & Associates as he'd have liked. In turn the finances had suffered.

Furthermore, Jennifer knew that Quinter had been angry and hurt by Natalie's unchallengeable decision to send the boy off to Exeter the summer before his lower middle year. He had responded by spending most of his free time either with his son or in a sudden renewed interest in the gym and physical conditioning. He had tried, almost desperately, she thought, to share everything in an effort to develop intimacy with his son. And she understood Quinter missed watching his son grow, and that he longed for the opportunity to reassert his influence upon the young man's direction and life.

These negatives in Quinter's life had been obvious to Jennifer, if not to others. He had become less carefree and less confident. He also had become physically and emotionally distant. By the early spring of 1987, Jennifer and Quinter were seeing each other socially only on occasion. Any discussion of living together had long since ceased, and the mention of a more intimate and stable situation made Quinter defensive and angry. The relationship had limped to an end.

On the other hand, as a partial consolation, Jennifer's work had been absorbing. She had taken responsibility for establishing business systems including billing, and had set up a rudimentary docket department which tracked law cases through the courts. She began to experiment with the use of computers not only in word processing for legal briefs and court pleadings, but also with the new office systems she had developed. She understood computers could be valuable for record keeping, tracking efficiency, and evaluating profitability, and she enjoyed harnessing their power to assist her in solving problems and tracing history.

Furthermore she liked working with Quinter's clients and made a special effort to know them in person, especially if there was even an outside chance for repeat work.

Over the past five months, however, the intimate relationship that she and Quinter had begun at Davis-James had eroded into a hollow, impersonal, business relationship.

What made this increasingly difficult for her to bear was her late-blooming discovery that she was in love with him. That he could not, or would not, reciprocate her feelings troubled her so greatly that she eventually determined that their relationship would not continue in its present form. She would either succeed in recapturing the joy and passion of their former relationship, or she would move elsewhere and rebuild her life.

The trip to Spain would be her last effort to rekindle their romance.

"Jenny, I'm back. Where are you?" Quinter opened the bedroom door. "Jeff and Martha are cooking 'lobsta' for dinner and we are to be the beneficiaries! And can you believe that when I dropped your photograph off at the gate they knew me by name? I never met the guy before, but he recognized me. Anyhow, are you ready?"

Quinter was wearing the new herringbone sport jacket he'd bought "off the shelf" that afternoon, which by some miracle fit him, as did the new brown slacks and yellow button down pinpoint oxford dress shirt. He looked comfortable and casual—even somehow elegant—and was in obvious good spirits.

"I'm ready," she replied standing up from the dressing table. While collecting her thoughts she adjusted the green cashmere sweater so that it hugged the shape of her body, and straightened her skirt.

"Shall we?" she stated.

"Shall we what?" Quinter inquired in a mocking manner. "You look fetching," he added.

"Shall we go?" she said flatly, but turned away to hide her smile.

"Oh, why yes. Yes, of course," he teased, "let's go."

The sun was trending lower in the sky as they headed south to pick up the road to Gloucester. Traffic was light and Quinter was able to proceed at a fairly steady forty-five miles per hour, and within as many minutes they were on the out-skirts of the city, looking for the Red Eagle market and then the dirt road leading to his friend's summer home. Quinter found the driveway without difficulty, and turned in, passing through an open gate in the white picket fence which sur-rounded the Downing's property.

Jeff and Martha were sitting on the front porch. When Jeff got up to throw a stick for Lolly, their golden retriever, he saw the car coming up the driveway and broke into a grin. He took Martha by the hand, and walked to meet the car. Quinter and Jennifer got out and walked toward the approaching couple.

When the two men met, they hugged, simultaneously thumping each other on the back in audible whacks.

"Wonderful to see you Jeff . . . and Martha. . ." Quinter did not finish the sentence, but grasped Martha by the shoulders and kissed her on the cheek affectionately. "I'd like you to meet Jennifer Millieux."

After the introductions, the group went inside the house where Jennifer and Quinter met the Downing's' six year old son, Jamie, and daughter Elyse, age two. The two children soon made fast friends with Jennifer who joined in their tag and other games on the back lawn while Martha put the finishing touches on her full-fledged New England lobster dinner.

Settled in on the front porch enjoying a stiff martini, Quinter and Jeff quickly got caught up. Then Quinter told Jeff of his meeting with Bordman at Cafe Angeles, and gave him a detailed description of all that had occurred afterward.

72

Jeff listened intently, his eyebrows occasionally furrowing in thought.

"I must say that you've accepted an interesting proposal," Jeff began, "but, I have reservations about this Nortex outfit. There are more than a few people who believe Nortex is too powerful and would have no problem putting its goals and methods above the law."

Jeff got up from his rocker and walked over to the porch railing. "You may remember the charge made a couple of years back by Senator Davis, you know, the crusty Ranking Member of the Senate Foreign Relations Committee, that Nortex made large illegal profits from several government contracts by falsifying amounts for labor and materials, and worse yet, several side deals with some pretty unsavory regimes. Johnson was subjected to a real grilling by one of the Senate subcommittees. Not a very contrite man to say the least."

Jeff took a sip of his drink and then placed the glass on the railing beside him. "But for Johnson's pal, Senator James, the Committee Chair, I think they would have hung him on the spot.

"In any event, when the press got involved and the matter began to stink to high heaven, the Pentagon was forced to withhold payments in the millions. The company quickly agreed to settle with the Justice Department, which as I recall, meant a fine of three-quarters of a million bucks."

"I remember reading about the fine," Quinter said.

"That's not an unusual defense contractor story these days," Jeff went on, "but the people that I know at Justice who struck the deal concluded there were more than one of your proverbial 'bad apples' in the Nortex barrel."

"I get your point, Jeff. From what little I know about this venture, I think the Nortex people are at least flirting with involvement in matters which are covered by U.S.

foreign policy. However, Bordman made a point of telling me their role in the Spanish deal was by express invitation from State."

"Could be," Jeff added, while nodding. "Tom, do you remember Harry Dunkirk in the class behind us at Michigan?"

"Sure," Quinter responded. "He was the guy who always wore dark glasses to our 8:00 o'clock Business Associations class so Professor James couldn't tell when he drifted off for a short snooze. Scared the hell out of him one day when James left the lectern, walked up the aisle to his seat and yelled 'Good morning!' in his ear," recounted Quinter, and the two men enjoyed a good laugh. "I liked him, but I think you knew him better than I," he continued.

"We became friends, and since we left school I've seen him a number of times, both in Boston and in Washington when I was on the Nicaragua-Honduras boundary mess."

Jeff picked up his drink from the railing, took another sip, and returned to the rocker. "Tom, Harry Dunkirk is one of the fellows at Justice who does not have a high opinion of your employer. In fact, he thinks they're crooks. And he has a particular dislike for your old friend, Bordman. Says he would steal from his grandmother."

"He may be right," replied Quinter. "But I'm giving Dave a pass until I have good reason to change my opinion of him from basically good to *maybe* bad."

"Well, that's fair, but," Jeff went on, "you should know that Harry worked for the Nortex law department in New York before going with Justice. According to the buzz, he was fired for being the next thing to a whistle-blower, and Nortex blackballed him in the private legal community. So, there's no love lost."

"Interesting," mused Quinter. "You know Jeff, there may come a time when I need your help."

"Anytime buddy, at two hundred an hour," said Jeff in a flip manner to belie his affection.

"That's right. I forgot. You're in the big leagues now," Quinter grinned, knowing he'd be able to count on Jeff as a trusted friend at any time.

"Jennifer is very nice," began Jeff, changing the subject and then lapsing into chatter about his family.

But Quinter's thoughts, at the mention of Jennifer's name, had gone elsewhere, the phrase 'big leagues' somehow taking him back.

I<small>T WAS A</small> beautiful late summer afternoon in 1985. The day was blue and clear, a perfect day for the annual Davis-James picnic. As Quinter neared the baseball diamond, he stopped to fish a cold beer out of a convenient cooler. He could hear laughter and applause. Mr. Davis had just hit a grounder between third and short and was on his way to first as the outfielder got to the ball, much to the cheers of the assembled crowd.

Quinter took a long draught of his beer, and looked at Natalie, who was playing third. She was absorbed in the game, and oblivious to the occasional puff of wind, which blew her shoulder-length blond hair across her finely chiseled face.

Quinter took another swig of beer. His mind drifted to the face of Judge Lambert who had sternly delivered his charge to the jury the previous afternoon. "You are the sole judges of the facts and you must determine if the plaintiff has sustained its case against the defendants by the greater weight of the credible evidence," Judge Lambert had cautioned the jury. Less than three hours later, having dutifully deliberated, the jury found that the plaintiff company had not sustained the burden of proof, and Quinter recorded his seventh consecutive courtroom win.

Quinter's attention was attracted by shouts of indignation coming from the volleyball game behind him. He turned to his left in time to see his secretary Jennifer throw her hands up in the air in a gesture of utter hopelessness. Jim Drake, a new associate who had 'volunteered' as referee, was standing by his decision that the shot had landed out of bounds, ending the game. In spite of the angry reaction, he was not to be deterred from pronouncing the truth as he saw it.

The image of Jennifer lingered with Quinter and he felt a familiar arousal. He walked behind the backstop toward the volleyball net to look at her. Jennifer wore cut-off jeans frayed at mid-thigh and a man's white shirt knotted by its shirttails in front, leaving bare her sun-bronzed waist.

Natalie, from her position at third base, became aware of Quinter's distraction and watched him leave the diamond and walk toward the volleyball game.

Damn him, she thought. *I don't need him anymore. And I don't want him anymore.* She could scarcely believe what she was thinking. Had these buried emotions become sharp enough to come to the surface? In a succeeding weak moment the thought flashed into her head that perhaps she should become pregnant again—she knew how badly he wanted another child—and just as quickly rejected the idea. As her eyes squinted with determination at the left-handed batter at the far side of home plate, she felt empty.

Jennifer surreptitiously glanced at Quinter who was now standing beside one of the net poles. He was looking at her, and her cheeks turned crimson. Without thinking, she straightened her shoulders and thrust her chest forward in a purposely sensuous motion, then bending to rub the back of her right thigh. While maintaining this pose, she slowly turned her head in his direction and engaged his eyes, smiling provocatively. Quinter responded without thought.

"Jennifer," he called, "let's take a walk."

They began walking down the dry dusty access road that separated the baseball field from the makeshift volleyball court, heading deeper into the park and facing the lake below. Once out of sight, Quinter, who had said little, slipped his arm around Jennifer's bare waist. She stopped, turned toward him, and placing her arms around his back, gently but firmly pulled him close to her. Warmth and electricity began to flow between their bodies.

"Oh Tom . . ." she murmured in his ear, her lips brushing his earlobe. "I've been waiting so long for you to hold me in your arms."

"Jenny . . . you feel so good," Quinter responded, as the scent of her hair and pressure of her body increased his arousal.

"Tell me what you want," Jennifer breathed into Quinter's ear. "Tell me what you need . . ."

"I want you, Jenny. I need you," Quinter whispered between short gasps for breath.

"Show me," Jennifer urged him, slipping her hands around his neck and pulling his head toward her now upturned face. "I want you as much as you want me," she said, and the couple embraced long, hard, and passionately.

Fifty yards away up the dusty road and concealed by the lush green foliage, Natalie turned her back to the two people now merged in passionate embrace. She dropped to one knee, placing her face in her hands and cried softly. Her temples were pounding and waves of nausea interspersed with raw anger flooded through her body.

Then fury took full control. No, she did not need that son of a bitch any longer. He could go straight to hell and scorch for eternity, and her father might just be willing to help him get there.

"Tom, Tom. Hello Tom! Are you there?" Jeff's direct question restored Quinter's focus.

"Sorry, Jeff," answered Quinter. "I was lost."

"Lobsta' time," called Martha from the far side of the front porch.

"And it smells heavenly," added Jennifer.

"What a sweet family," Jennifer sighed, as Quinter turned off the dirt road to onto State Route 133 for the return trip to Haverhill. "And the food . . . incredible. I'm stuffed."

"Agreed," said Quinter, "and it was great to see Jeff and Martha."

As the miles to Haverhill sped by, Quinter told Jennifer about the days at Michigan law where he first met Jeff. "You know, Jenny, Jeff and I had some great times together at Michigan. We both worked the dish washer crew in Hutchins. Had a lot of fun and got the best steaks in the house! By the way, have you ever been in a football stadium with a hundred thousand and one crazy people?"

"I've been to lots of games, but I don't think with that many," replied Jennifer, sensing that Quinter needed to talk.

"Well," continued Quinter "Jeff and I spent many a beautiful Saturday afternoon along with ninety nine thousand nine hundred and ninety nine others at the Michigan stadium. You wouldn't believe the noise! Almost unbearable."

"It's hard to picture that many people at a game," Jennifer replied.

"I also remember when Jeff and I were swimming at a small lake in the northern part of the Upper Peninsula," Quinter continued, his mind drifting. "Jeff tired in the middle of the lake, and I helped him. He told me he'd never have been able to reach the shore by himself. I was scared as hell, because I was getting pretty tired myself. Something passed between us, Jenny, that made our friendship special. I think I grew up a little that day because I had become a real part of another man's life."

Jennifer listened intently. She enjoyed hearing Quinter speak of personal matters, and for the first time in many months felt she was with him again as a partner.

She looked at him closely. He seemed younger than his chronological age of forty-two, yet when he was relaxed, slight visible lines appeared etched in his forehead. When he was perplexed or angry, which was seldom, furrows stood out on his brow, and vertical wrinkles occurred just above his eyebrows. His eyes were gray, and he had a large shock of blond hair, parted on the right that was forever falling over his forehead. An interesting-looking man, thought Jennifer, not pretty, but interesting, perhaps even handsome.

"Jeff also told me several stories about Nortex." Quinter began again. "Had some unpleasant words for Bordman. All hearsay, mind you, but based upon fairly reliable sources."

"From what I can tell, Jeff's a perceptive person," answered Jennifer. "And Tom, I do sense a coldness in Bordman that makes me uneasy. Nothing specific, but he's so damn goal-oriented. Sometimes I wonder if he has any boundaries."

"I know what you mean," replied Quinter, softly as he brought the car to a stop at the Nortex security gate.

"Good evening, Mr. Quinter. Mr. Bordman left a message for you that he'll meet you at the cafeteria in the Rotunda tomorrow at 12:30. Seems he's had a slight delay."

"Thanks," Quinter replied," are there any new unauthorized areas since this morning?"

79

"Not to my knowledge, Mr. Quinter," said the young uniformed officer trying unsuccessfully to suppress a laugh, "but I just work the gate."

"Have a nice evening," said Quinter as he pulled the car away from the entrance and turned left heading toward the guest quarters.

Quinter parked the car for the evening in the lot opposite the entrance. As they walked down the hall Quinter grasped Jennifer's hand and they proceeded in silence. Jennifer trembled at his touch. He opened the door and after closing it, secured the dead bolt and chain.

"Let's have a nightcap, Jenny."

"OK," she replied. "Let me freshen up a bit," and she walked toward her bedroom closing the door behind her.

Jennifer sat down on the bed and crossing her hands in front of her grasped the bottom of her sweater pulling it over her head in a single gesture. She unbuttoned her cotton blouse, allowing it to fall behind her on the bed. She bent over to free her breasts from the lace-trimmed brassiere and working the back around in front of her, released the hooks dropping it on top of the sweater.

She stood up, walked to the dressing table and brushed her hair, laying it smoothly over her shoulders. She picked up the small bottle of Madame Rochas cologne and placed a drop between her breasts and on her neck behind her ears. From the dresser drawer, she took a bright red silk nightshirt, pulled it over her head, removed her panty hose, and put on a pair of red high-heeled pumps.

Returning to the dressing table, she reddened her lips with lipstick and started toward the living room door, pausing before the full-length mirror to adjust the nightshirt so that it fell evenly over the top of her thighs. The neckline of the nightshirt stopped just short of the outline of her nipples and revealed the full curve of her firm breasts. It hugged the lines of her hips and flattered her long well-shaped legs.

Satisfied with her appearance and newly confident, she left her room and walked toward Quinter who was sitting on the sofa.

As she left the bedroom, Quinter followed her every movement. She was lovely and sensual. She stopped in front of him, kneeling down on one knee. She took his head in her hands, and began kissing his lips, at first lightly and then gradually with more pressure, while flickering her tongue against the inside of his lips.

Feeling the sensuous pleasure and keenly aware of his growing erection, Quinter arose from the sofa, lifted her in his arms, and carried her to his bedroom. He sat her on the bed, and after unbuttoning his shirt and throwing it on the chair, clumsily removed his pants.

Then he sat next to her and began sliding the silky material over her firm buttocks, cupping her waist with his hands, and finally up over her shoulders. She shuddered as the cool silk and then his hot touch moved over her body.

The nightshirt removed, he reclined her full length on her side and back so that they were looking at each other. He lay down next to her and they held each other tightly, and then began stroking toward arousal, first in tension and then in mutual release and satisfaction.

"It's been so long, Tom," murmured Jennifer.

"*Too* long Jenny." sighed Quinter, and they drifted to sleep in each other's arms.

7

OFF TO SPAIN

THE SUN WAS WELL UP when Quinter awoke. He looked over at Jennifer, still asleep. She was beautiful and serene, strong and full of life.

"Good morning, honey," he said as he kissed her gently on the right cheek, smoothing back her hair.

"Mmmm . . .," she said sleepily, without opening her eyes.

"Let's check out the pool," continued Quinter as he turned his head and, leaning on one elbow, looked out the window. "It's a beautiful day, Jenny, and we're going to Spain tonight," he said, almost exuberantly.

"Lovely," she sighed as she pulled on her red nightshirt. She combed her hair with her fingers, while adjusting to Quinter's energetic mood. "I'll get my suit and meet you in the living room." Jennifer arose from the bed and walked toward the bathroom that connected their rooms.

When she reached the door, she stopped and turning her head back toward Quinter who was watching her from the bed said, "Tom, I had a wonderful evening. Let's not wait so long for the next time."

Quinter nodded, while following her every step until she disappeared from view. He felt peaceful and secure. The twisted hurtful days and lonely nights at the end of his professional relationship with Davis-James, and the petty meanness of his separation and divorce from Natalie, seemed but a faded snapshot of someone else's melodrama. For the first time in many months, he felt ready to set a new course. *She's tough and a great lover,* he thought, *What a combination. I'm glad she agreed to come.*

Quinter's body shattered the surface of the water causing a thousand ripples. Still underwater, he opened his eyes and followed the reflections of the sun as they danced on the blue tile bottom toward the far end of the pool. The water was refreshingly cool as he relaxed and settled into a steady crawl. In a short time he had completed his fifteenth lap.

Jennifer, seated in one of the recliners brushing the snarls from her wet hair, watched him make a racing flip-turn at the end of the pool. As she did, she replayed in her mind the intimacy they had shared the night before. *No,* she smiled to herself, *it would not be long until the next time.*

At half past twelve, Quinter and Jennifer met Bordman for lunch in the Nortex dining room located on the first floor of the Rotunda. When they arrived, Bordman beckoned to them from his seat at the far end of the room.

The maître d' appeared. "You will be joining Mr. Bordman . . ." he said in a half-questioning statement as he began escorting the couple toward Bordman's table.

"Good afternoon, Dave," Quinter offered.

"Tom. Jennifer. Have a seat," Bordman replied. "Young Joel Johnson will be joining us. It's his twenty-third birthday today. He's been celebrating with daddy who assured me earlier he was going to try to put some steel into the boy. Got a ways to go."

84

Jennifer and Quinter sat down as the waiter poured two goblets of ice water and set a wooden pallet with half a loaf of French bread in the center of the table. He handed menus to the group and laid an additional one on the white linen table cloth in front of the empty chair.

"Joel appeared upset the other night," Jennifer said to Bordman. "It seemed almost as if he was being required to do something he believed was dangerous or perhaps even wrong. Is there a problem?"

"Not that I know of," answered Bordman coolly. "He's just a kid. Here he comes now."

Joel Johnson walked into the main dining room. He was wearing a charcoal gray sweater, which covered all but the knot of his Brooks Brother's rep tie.

"Hello Joel," Bordman began in his usual authoritative tone," How's Duane?"

"He's fine, Mr. Bordman. Hello, Miss Millieux, Mr. Quinter. I guess we leave tonight."

"That's the plan," said Bordman, "We meet with the Spanish Minister of Defense in two days. I hear he's had people shot for sneezing."

"Sounds like a difficult fellow," responded Quinter calmly, while noting a hint of fear flicker across the younger Johnson's face.

"Happy birthday, Joel," Jennifer and Quinter offered almost simultaneously.

"Thanks." Joel replied.

"I have some more information about Reynolds' murder," continued Bordman in a matter-of-fact tone that betrayed no emotion. "Seems one of the Iraqis outwitted the Boston police and hung himself by his belt in his cell at city jail. Damn fools should have known better than to give the creep a way out. When they found him, his face was purple."

Joel choked audibly on the ice water, using his napkin to wipe his chin.

"Get a grip, kid. Happens all the time," Bordman continued with more than a hint of meanness in his voice.

"The cops grilled the other Iraqi for several hours. He belongs to some sort of small fundamentalist Muslim sect that apparently hates Iranians and anyone helping them. He rambled on about genocide and something about the recent murder of his mother and younger brother during an Iranian cross-border tank attack."

The waiter returned and took the lunch orders, disappearing as unobtrusively as he had appeared.

"The police obtained no information as to why the two men selected Sir Bertram as their target," Bordman continued as if there had been no interruption. "They expect it will be some time before we get a full explanation, if ever."

"Are they sure they caught the right people," inquired Quinter?

"Well, they did a spectrographic analysis on the silver paint removed from the rental vehicle," answered Bordman, "and the sample matched the paint from Sir Bertram's Bentley. Didn't find a weapon. There was no confession, but there's little question those two birds did it."

The waiter reappeared and served the table.

"Your father told me you are to be the company spokesman and coordinator, Joel," said Quinter.

"I think, Mr. Quinter, he meant I would keep him advised. Mr. Bordman's going to run the operation," replied young Johnson in a differential tone.

"Well," interjected Bordman, "I'm glad we see this eye to eye."

Joel, head down toward his half-eaten lunch, did not reply.

"Don't be too tough, Dave," Quinter responded. "Save it for the Spaniards."

"Someone's got to do the dirty work, Tom," replied Bordman, "and I can't say I appreciate having someone looking over my shoulder."

"Why David," chided Quinter, "if I didn't know you better, I'd think you were insecure."

"You know, Tom," said Bordman firmly, "each of us has a job to do, and I've never liked to be second-guessed."

"Dave, I doubt if anyone is second-guessing you—or would dare to," Quinter replied, letting a little too much truth into his add-on. Finishing the last of his meal, Quinter turned to Jennifer. "If you're finished, Jenny, would you like to take a walk? It's a beautiful day."

"That's a nice idea, Tom. I'm ready if you are. Would you excuse us?" she asked, turning to Joel and Bordman.

"Of course," answered Bordman, "It is a good day for a stroll. By the way, Felix will pick you both up at about 7:15 this evening. We'd like to be in the air by 8:00."

"We'll be ready," said Quinter as he and Jennifer stood up. "See you tonight."

Jennifer and Quinter walked out of the Rotunda into the bright sunshine. As they passed the two guards on duty at the front entrance, Quinter turned to Jennifer, and asked, "What did you make of our lunch?"

"A little unnerving. Also, Bordman seemed downright hostile toward Joel," she answered.

"I thought so too," commented Quinter, as they began walking down the long diagonal sidewalk.

The remainder of the day passed quickly, as Quinter and Jennifer spent a large portion of it enjoying one another. He seemed, to her, to have rediscovered the lost intimacy they once had. She sensed a possible renewal of their relationship, at the same time wondering if it were only wishful thinking on her part. Nonetheless, for the moment she felt secure in the warmth of his affectionate attention. Her eyes were bright, and she laughed and smiled easily.

A little after 7:00, Quinter picked up the two new suitcases from the sofa, and carried them down the hall to the front entrance of the guest residence. He placed them near the door on the porch. Jennifer followed, carrying a suit bag and a small leather traveling case which she had bought in Haverhill the day before. She pushed open the front door and walked over to Quinter who was standing at the top of the steps. In a few minutes the limousine entered the security gate. Within a few more, Felix had loaded the luggage in the trunk and the limo started back out through the gate toward the airport.

"Well, here goes nothing," Quinter whispered to Jennifer.

"O.K.," Jennifer answered softly, then grasping Quinter's hand. "Let's roll the dice."

"Onward and upward!" said Quinter, even while thinking, *She likes the excitement and daring almost as much as I do. Looks like we might make a good team . . . I think we're going to need one. . .*

At the Haverhill airport Felix followed the signs announcing "Departing Flights". He parked the limo in front of the entrance, and the three people, luggage in tow, walked inside past the empty ticket counters to the pilot's lounge. A flight services attendant was sitting in one of the lounge chairs across from the desk.

"Good evening," she said with a smile," Nortex?"

"Yes, ma'am," Felix answered.

"Second door on the right, out the ramp and to your left," she said gesturing toward the area.

"Thank you, ma'am," said Felix who knew exactly where he was going.

On the ramp, the Gulfstream G4 sat gleaming. Beams of late afternoon sunlight reflecting off the top of the plane forced the group to look down at the tarmac. Within moments, the forward boarding ladder, the large red letters spelling out Nortex, and the gold corporate coat-of-arms depicting the struggling men came into view, and one by one the group climbed aboard.

Inside the aircraft, the first two rows were individual leather reclining chairs. Quinter saw that the seats were more amply spaced than in a normal first class cabin, and that they swiveled so occupants in different rows could face one another. In the center area, two more rows of facing seats were located on one side, and on the other, there was a small plush bronze leather sofa. In the rear section of the cabin, two final rows bracketed a black walnut table, and here Bordman sat talking to Graham Butler and Cornelius Tester. The men were dressed casually.

"Good evening," offered Quinter.

"Evening," responded Bordman.

"Jones and young Johnson will be joining us soon," Bordman continued. Felix worked to stow the baggage and after completing the task turned to Bordman and Quinter, inquiring whether they needed anything else. Upon receiving a negative response, he excused himself and deplaned.

"Accommodating fellow, and very nice," commented Quinter as he took the open seat next to Bordman while Jennifer seated herself to his right.

"Yes, and also efficient," replied Bordman, a wry smile on his face. He drained the last of the Absolute he'd been drinking. "Anyone else?" he asked, almost slurring his words as he reached for the bottle on the table in front of him.

"Don't mind if I do," replied Tester taking a glass from a rack under the table and filling it halfway with ice from the container which had been placed next to the bottle.

"A little nip will help pass the time. How long is the trip to Lisbon?" Bordman asked, looking at Quinter.

"Seven hours is a pretty good guess," replied Quinter, his attention drawn toward the sound of voices coming through the open hatch in the front of the aircraft.

Shortly, Joel Johnson and Ralph Jones entered carrying their luggage, which they stowed in the forward baggage compartment before joining the group. After a moment, an attendant appeared and said,

"We will be taxiing for take-off position, and I would ask that you take a seat. Once the captain has turned off the seat-belt sign, you may get up and walk around the cabin if you'd like. And you can take your drinks with you," he said.

Jennifer and Quinter took a seat on the starboard side of the aircraft on the small sofa just in front of the wing. Although she had said nothing, Quinter thought she probably wanted to see outside so he guided her into the best position. He sat next to her, arching backward to straighten his back. Across the aisle Graham Butler was sitting by himself. Tester and Jones were seated several rows behind Butler, and Bordman and Johnson sat in front.

"It's hard to believe we're on our way to Spain," Jennifer sighed as she placed her left hand on Quinter's shoulder.

"It does seem a little surreal," he replied with a smile. He glanced at Jennifer thinking how pretty she looked with her face reddened by slight sunburn and her auburn hair settling on the shoulders of her tan turtleneck sweater.

"That was wonderful last night—I love you baby," he said reaching across and grasping her right hand with his and kissing her on the left temple.

"I love you too, Tom. Let's make it that kind of trip."

Quinter bent his head toward her. Their lips met, lightly at first and then more firmly with stirrings of passion. The embrace ended and the couple looked at each other, smiling, and then breaking into a quiet laugh. No, it would not be so long until the next time, they each thought, knowing the thought was shared.

The intimacy of their mood was disturbed by the increasing whine of the engines gulping for air as the pilot applied take-off power. Slowly at first, and then with gathering speed the nose inched higher and the aircraft accelerated down the runway. At climb attitude the craft made a smooth lift-off and the setting sun seemed to reverse its direction for a few brief moments until the pilot entered a right bank, heading east over the Atlantic Ocean.

8

FROG FOUNTAIN

THE SCREECH OF THE RUBBER wheels against the tarmac and the jostling of the aircraft as it struggled against the inevitability of being once again earthbound woke Quinter from a restless sleep.

"Good morning, love," said Jennifer quietly. Quinter narrowed his eyes to avoid the bright daylight flooding in through the half-drawn curtains. He looked at his watch. 4:30. He reset it to 10:30.

"Good morning, Jenny. What day is it?"

"Sunday," she replied fighting back a yawn, "Sunday in Madrid."

"Good morning, Tom," said Graham Butler from across the aisle, "Nice day for a nap." The two men laughed easily together. Quinter had enjoyed their conversation during the flight after Jennifer had fallen asleep. He had been drawn to the quiet straight-ahead methodology of Butler's thought process, much as Butler admired the electric leaps by which

Quinter's proceeded. In a remarkably short period of time, a bond of trust had developed between the two men.

"UNDERSTAND YOU HAVE a son at Exeter," Butler had begun earlier on the flight.

"Yeah," Quinter answered. "He's a Lower Middler, second year."

"I have a boy, Dan, who's a freshman. His coach told me he has some promise as a hurdler. He spends a lot of time in the cage," continued Butler referring to the school's indoor athletic facility.

"Interesting," answered Quinter. "My son runs the 100 and 220. Bet they practice together."

"I'm sure they do," replied Butler.

He paused, and then began again, "You know, Tom, I don't think Sir Bertram's death was a random isolated murder. As of now, I suspect that it may have been planned by some misguided crazies who don't want Spain to be drawn deeper into NATO. Johnson says the police are focused on this extremist sect thing, but I'm not sure we have the whole story."

"Really?" said Quinter thoughtfully. "After Bordman asked me to do this job for Nortex, someone trashed my law office and attacked Jennifer." Butler listened attentively as Quinter related the details.

"Well, Tom, I think that you are a square shooter, and I believe you are entitled to know that I think something is going on. I'm supposed to be in charge of all security for the operation. Yet the details are given to me on a need-to-know basis and I'm not sure I'm getting all that I should be getting. So I'm troubled. I don't know how the hell I am going to protect the company if I'm not getting full information. In my book, your story adds fuel to the fire, and could be a connection. What do you know about Nortex's new energy division?"

"Not much," answered Quinter. "But I've done a little looking and learned Energia doesn't own any energy-producing facilities. No coal reserves. No oil. No nothing."

"That's true. Energia seems to be involved in some type of shipping operation. Shipping was Sir Bertram's strength, although nobody ever talked about it at the company. In fact, the only information I have is that Energia purchased some new oil tankers, two sister-ships, the *Middle Eastern Star* and the *Crescent*. They were built in the Lisbon shipyards. Big ones. Each has a dead-weight tonnage of about 165,000 tons, and is over 900 feet in length and 170 feet in beam, and draws about 55 feet of water—a classic tanker configuration. See, I've done a little looking too."

"Must have something to do with our stop in Lisbon, don't you think, Graham?"

"Probably. One of Jones's responsibilities is to check them out and make sure they're seaworthy."

More speculation produced no further answers, and the topic died before the aircraft touched down in Lisbon to deposit Ralph Jones, who deplaned without a word. He was met by two men wearing Nortex uniforms: dark blue gabardine with Nortex in red lettering over the left breast and the gold insignia on the right shoulder. Just minutes later, the pilot began to taxi for take-off and soon the aircraft was again airborne, heading toward the Spanish capitol.

Quinter and Butler continued their conversation, rejuvenated to some extent by Jones's departure. Butler confirmed Quinter's suspicion that Bordman had been drinking more than usual. He said this new behavior change had begun in the last six or eight months, and did not seem to be related to anything in particular. According to Butler, on a couple of occasions Bordman had drunk to the point where his control was in jeopardy, and while he never actually made a fool of himself, his conduct had been seen as borderline. "Nonetheless," Butler added, "he still remains very much Johnson's good right hand if 'good' is the right word."

Wɪᴛʜ ᴀ ғɪɴᴀʟ lurch and squeak of the brakes, the aircraft stopped at gate number 27 of the Madrid International airport. The customs agent asked only a few perfunctory questions, and in no time the group was walking through the domestic side of the terminal, headed toward the front entrance. Several hundred feet before they reached the entrance, Bordman turned to Jennifer and Quinter, and said, "We've made reservations for you at the Hotel Residencia Carlos V, Maestro Vitoria, 5. Five star it's not, but you'll find the place clean and equipped with all the necessary amenities."

He reached in the pocket of his trench coat, pulled out a large envelope and handed it to Quinter. "This contains all the information you will need, including our itinerary and the best way to reach us at any time. I also added an advance on your expenses in addition to the money I gave you on the plane.

"As general background, you should know we'll be staying at an apartment near the Royal Palace and then meeting at the office of the Minister of Defense tomorrow at 10:00. That's it. Cabs are out in front and to the left. Let's go."

As they walked toward the exit, Quinter noticed a young man, phone in hand, watching them from a bank of telephones. Dressed in a dark suit with a dull red tie he was holding a small briefcase under his left arm. When Quinter's eyes engaged his, he smiled and continued talking, but then turned away.

As they reached the entrance of the airport, Quinter saw a number of people carrying signs and walking on the front sidewalk. Some of the women were holding small children. A line of federal police, standing several yards apart, separated the picketers from the doors. On some of the signs Quinter was able to pick out the word NATO. He turned to Jennifer and asked, "What's their problem?"

"The sign in front of you and to your right says 'NATO is not consistent with independence and freedom for Spain' and the one behind and further to the left loosely translates to 'More weapons only increases the chances our children will be killed in a war that is not ours.'" Quinter nodded.

The Nortex group continued to walk through the open space between the police officers and the terminal building, heading for the cab stand. When they arrived, Bordman looked at Quinter and said, "I told you about difficulties in the weapons deal. These idiots are a part of the problem. Several European representatives to NATO will be arriving in an hour or so, and these people would be delighted to stir up trouble.

"There's a TV cameraman," Boardman continued, pointing beyond the picket line, "whose tape, I am sure, will be used to play up the protest for the evening news."

"Thomas, you and Jennifer take the first cab. I'll be hearing from you in a day or so. Good luck."

"So long, Dave," replied Quinter and the two men shook hands.

Jennifer and Quinter climbed into the taxi. "Hotel Carlos Quinto," said Jennifer. The cab left the stand and merged into the traffic pattern leaving the Madrid airport.

THE LATE SUNDAY morning was warm and clear. People were parading in their finery. The women were dressed in every conceivable color, many wearing gowns with embroidery and sequins and the men displaying their Sunday best from formal attire to business casual.

The cab, by now weaving at a greater than necessary pace through the light traffic, had already only narrowly avoided crashing several stop lights. Finally, the driver, gesturing in a display of utter frustration, screeched to a stop at a full red light, but only because the vehicle in front of him had stopped.

Quinter looked out the window to his left. Just beyond a street sign that read 'Puerta del Sol' was a statue of a surprisingly muscular bear rising on his haunches with his forepaws on the trunk of a tree nibbling at the tender under-leaves. To Quinter's right, he could see a series of fountains gracefully spraying plumes of water into the air, when his view was partially blocked by a black sedan. In the front passenger's seat was the man he had seen on the telephone at the airport.

The man gave no indication that he was aware of the cab and its passengers, and continued looking straight ahead.

The light turned green and the car in front of the cab started quickly, their cab driver following equally as fast. Not to be outdone, at the first available instant, the cabby pulled into the right lane, narrowly avoiding a parked motorcycle, and executing a perfect allie-oop, passed the car whose driver had shown a lack of good judgment by stopping at the previous red light.

To Quinter's and Jennifer's fascination–and no little fear– after asserting his rightful lead for several blocks, the driver made a swift right turn and in several hundred feet pulled to a jolting stop in front of the Carlos V, just as the black sedan passed by on the cross street.

The Carlos V was a pleasant, although not ostentatious, hotel. Quinter and Jennifer followed the bellhop through the tidily furnished lobby to the front desk. Just before reaching it, Quinter grasped Jennifer by her right arm.

Handing her the credit card, he said, quietly in her right ear, "I think a single room with a large bed will do just fine, don't you?"

With a smile, Jennifer nodded her agreement. Following the couples' brief conversation with the desk clerk, the bellhop escorted them to a room on the third floor facing out on a lane which passed by the side of the hotel. Jennifer said *"Gracias,"* tipping him as he was leaving.

"We're going to have a lot of fun, Jenny," said Quinter drawing her closely to him.

"I'm having a wonderful time already," she said as she tilted her face up toward his, and they kissed. "I'm going to take a quick shower and I'll meet you in bed in a moment," she said. She picked up the smaller of the two suitcases, and pushing one of the two chairs out of the way with her hip, laid it on the coffee table.

Quinter walked over to the window and pulled the curtains together barring much of the daylight. He took off his clothes and lay down on the bed pulling the covers over him.

Jennifer started toward the bathroom. In a few minutes she returned wearing the red nightshirt, but found Quinter dead asleep. "Oh my big strong man," she sighed with a smile. She got into bed beside him, placed her left arm around him, and, holding on to his right shoulder with her hand, fell asleep.

A s QUINTER AWOKE, he became aware of the warmth of Jennifer's body and that her face was resting, partly on his left shoulder and partly on the pillow underneath.

"Jenny. Jenny," he said softly, brushing her hair away from her eyes. "Time to wake up. It's almost quarter to 5:00." Jennifer moaned softly as she fought through the haze of semi-consciousness.

"We need to eat," he continued persistently.

"Alright." Jennifer sighed sleepily while stretching, "Just give me a moment."

A half hour later Quinter and Jennifer left the room, walking hand-in-hand down the hallway toward the elevator. After leaving the hotel, they made a right turn onto the Calle de Preciados, a wide pedestrian promenade lined with every conceivable shop and store and with many fountains and greenery in the median.

While most of the stores were closed, restaurants were open and people were sitting at tables drinking coffee or eating. Quinter was surprised by the large number of people. Many were sitting on the benches near the fountains or on the edge of a fountain itself, some engaged in apparent serious conversation and others just watching the greater numbers passing by. Children were wading among the ripples made by the playing water and splashing one another with gleeful laughs.

Quinter and Jennifer fell into the slow meandering pace of Sunday evening in Madrid, spurred on only by an occasional good-natured grumble from Quinter that a particular food looked or smelled good. After they'd walked a couple of blocks, Quinter spotted an empty table in the rear of an outdoor dining area and they sat down. A waiter appeared, dressed in black tie without jacket, and soon they were served.

"On the plane, I had an interesting conversation with Butler while you were sleeping," began Quinter, using a blue checkered napkin to wipe his mouth clean of the last of his chicken.

"He thinks something is going on that Nortex security and most of the company know nothing about. As far as he can tell, the Energia Division is a shell—the division's only assets are a couple of brand new oil tankers which are being retrofitted."

Jennifer looked up from her plate quizzically. "We know that the company has a weapons arrangement with Spain," she said.

"Yes, that's true," Quinter continued, "but Butler seems to believe there's more. And, reading between the lines, I get the impression he suspects there may be something questionable, even illegal, occurring. In any event, he's clearly worried. Well, enough of this. Shall we take a little stroll?"

"Sounds fine," Jennifer answered, "But first, I'm going to the ladies' room. I'll meet you over by the frog fountain." Quinter followed her gaze and saw that indeed there was a fountain decorated with frogs of various sizes, each one sitting on a lily pad with a stream of water coming from its mouth following an arc to meet at the center of the pool.

"That's hard to miss," said Quinter with a smile as he stood up, leaving money on the table.

At the fountain, the frogs, carved out of black marble, were intricately detailed from the digits on their feet to the spots on their back. On the other side of the collecting pool a young couple was having a disagreement, their voices half drowned out by the splashing water. To his right he saw two women struggling to keep their barking dogs separated.

Before he actually noticed him Quinter felt the presence of a man next to him. As he snapped his head to the left, he felt a powerful grip on his left arm just above his elbow, and then a sharp jab above his left hip.

"Do not try anything foolish or by the grace of Allah I will shove this blade into your guts," said a soft steady voice in a thick Middle Eastern accent. "That's right. Easy. Easy. Now slowly around fountain and toward archway. We have some talk to make."

As they walked lock step along a diagonal across the plaza, Quinter began sizing up his adversary. The man was about his

101

height but heavier, and judging by the strength of the grasp, very strong.

The awkwardness of the lockstep made Quinter momentarily lose his balance, and the bite of the knife made him wince.

"No foolish Meester Qinter or you will spend much time getting better, or maybe not at all," growled the man in a forced whisper. The man and Quinter reached the wrought iron arch spanning the entrance to a playground filled with laughing children.

"Now this way, down street."

The narrow street had room for no more than one small vehicle to pass at a time. Buildings lined either side of the road, and it appeared to end in about a hundred feet, branching into a three-way intersection. The road, which had no streetlights, was deserted and darker than the plaza.

As they entered the street the man snarled," You take not our warning in U.S., Meester Qinter. Allah is angry and unforgiving." A door opened and an old woman walked out carrying a pail and mop. She came toward the men and then passed by giving no sign of noticing anything unusual.

They approached the narrow corner and Quinter knew he had very little time to act. His heart thumping wildly in anticipation, he bent forward at the waist feigning a cough, but then clenching his fist, drove his left elbow upward to the rear with as much force as he could.

He made solid contact, and heard the cracking of teeth. Quinter wheeled around. The man's head was thrown backward, his knees were sagging, and blood was spurting from his mouth. Pressing his advantage, Quinter drove the knuckles of his right hand sharply into his assailant's now exposed throat, causing a high-pitched wheeze followed by involuntary gurgles from his fractured voice box. To finish him off, Quinter delivered a powerful kick to the groin, and the man crashed into the side of the building. As he fell, his head struck a small stone gargoyle, before hitting the cobblestone pavement with a thud.

Quinter watched the growing pool of blood as it flowed from the man's mouth and nose, streaking his black beard with crimson before puddling in the mortar between the stones. He bent over and searched the convulsing body but found nothing. He glanced back up the street toward the plaza and saw that it was still deserted. Catching the gleam of the knife lying on the street, he picked up the weapon by the long slender blade, and placed it upside down in the inside breast pocket of his sport jacket.

"Jesus," he whistled under his breath, "And by the grace of Allah to you, you bastard."

Looking back furtively several times Quinter hurried past the children's playground. The street where the man was lying now appeared shadowy black in contrast to the brighter lights of the plaza. A group of children playing *boules*, cheered as the smallest of them drove the leader out of contention. Quinter approached the frog fountain, blending into the crowd, and spotted Jennifer waiting on the other side, her hands on her hips.

"Jenny," he called out, "let's go."

"Tom," she answered in anxious recognition," Where were you?"

"No time for questions, honey, let's go, *now*."

The force of Quinter's statement told Jennifer that immediate action was required. The couple began to retrace their steps toward the Carlos V mingling with the crowd as it meandered up along the boulevard.

As they walked, Quinter told Jennifer how he was taken at knife point across the plaza. She listened with growing anxiety as he described his escape, and her eyes widened in horror when he opened his jacket and displayed the slender point of the knife that extended several inches above his inside breast pocket.

In a short time the couple had returned to their room at the Carlos V.

"We'll take the 7:00 train to Malaga in the morning," said Quinter taking hold of the bureau. "Help me move this thing over in front of the door."

The two undressed, got into bed, and holding each other, fell asleep.

9

TROUBLE ON THE TRAIN—AND A LITTLE CLARITY...

STANDING AT THE HOTEL WINDOW, Quinter looked out at the apartment building across the street. The rain had drizzled to a fine mist and already the first stirrings of early Monday morning activity were evident.

In the still-gray dawn, a meat delivery truck had just pulled up to the sidewalk in front of the café on the corner, as several city workers, assisted by a man with a hose, began to sweep the street with long thatched brooms. Quinter's watch showed 6:15. He glanced at the knife on the bureau which was still lodged against the door, and shivered as he thought about his encounter.

"So," he murmured, "I now have a connection between Nortex and the assault on Jennifer." *But warning?* He thought,

Warning against what, and by whom? Was the event an attempt to dissuade me from working for Nortex? And if so, why?"

"Did you say something, Tom?" asked Jennifer as she put a large dollop of raspberry jam on the last piece of her croissant.

"That bastard who grabbed me last night said his people had tried to warn me. I can only guess he meant that the attack on you and the trashing of my office were warnings not to accept Bordman's offer. Someone must have known not only that Bordman intended to meet me in Cleveland but also something about his proposal. It doesn't make sense. Jenny, we should get moving if we are to make the 7:00 train. Give me a hand moving this bureau back, would you?"

Crowds had already filled the Madrid station, but the ticket lines moved rapidly. Quinter and Jennifer boarded the second-to-last car and sat down on the left side near the middle of the coach. Soon the train was moving across the broad Meseta tableland into the outskirts of Alcazar de San Juan. Through the window, Jennifer saw that even though the earth appeared dry, a seemingly contradictory patchwork of golden grain separated by large green plants divided the land which was further punctuated by isolated clumps of trees.

Although Jennifer and Quinter had been quiet since leaving the hotel, the silence was not uncomfortable. Jennifer knew that he was troubled and perhaps a little fearful, but she also knew he would repress both feelings. *He's probably wondering if it was a mistake to bring me along,* Jennifer thought. She found comfort, however, in Quinter's concern for her safety, remembering many days, and more nights, when his only reciprocation was emotional distance.

She turned her attention to him as he sat gazing at nothing in particular, his forehead wrinkled in thought.

"Something bothering you?" she said softly.

"Oh, not much, honey. But we *are* at a decisive point. You know, we can pull out right now, and maybe save ourselves a lot of trouble. But damn it, if Butler is right and Nortex is involved in something bad, we may be the only ones who can stop these people, or at least expose them. But I use the word 'we' advisedly, Jenny, because, I know you didn't bargain for this. And to tell the truth, neither did I."

"What do you think we should do, Tom?"

"I think we don't have any option *but* to continue. There'll be risk, but I assume from your question you've considered the danger part. Frankly, I'm glad to have your help. I just hope neither of us gets hurt . . ." Quinter's voice trailed off at the end of the sentence.

Leaving the flatland behind, the train began winding its way up and through the rolling foothills of the Betic Mountains. From time to time an outcropping of rock, isolated and severe in appearance, would jut 300 or 400 feet into the air. Frequently, a stone structure often with a tower crowned a summit looking out over the undulating hills below. The stone architecture served as a reminder of the days when the first line of defense was to make certain an enemy was discovered long before he was in position to attack.

Jennifer noticed Quinter's body stiffen as the railroad car door slammed closed.

"What, honey?" she asked.

"Jenny," Quinter nodded slightly toward the front of the car, "that man over there—is he the one who attacked you?" Jennifer, following his motion, turned and saw a short stocky man seated on the right aisle side of the row two seats from the restroom, facing them. His black hair was thick and in disorder. Jennifer's eyes widened and then narrowed.

"I can't be sure," she said, "but his hair and his build are similar. I don't have a clear memory of his face."

Quinter reached into his inside jacket pocket and took out a packet of cigars. Withdrawing one, he unwrapped the cellophane.

"Excuse me for a moment. I'm going to use the restroom."

Quinter got up and began walking down the aisle toward the front of the car, holding the cigar. Just before he came abreast of the man's seat, he stopped.

"You don't have a match do you, buddy?" The man had been looking down as Quinter approached, but the sound of the words made his head snap up. Then, surprised by the intensity of Quinter's stare, he looked down again.

"No hablo inglis," he said in a thick voice.

"A match, a match, buddy," Quinter said thrusting the cigar toward the man's face.

The man grunted something, and then reached inside his shirt pocket and pulled out a box of matches which he held out to Quinter. Quinter took the box, struck one and lit the cigar while continuing to look the man in the eyes.

"Ever been to America, buddy? Ever been to the U.S. of A.?"

Quinter jabbed the lit cigar toward the flinching man's face

"No hablo," the man protested under his breath.

"I'll bet you don't," continued Quinter, and with a smile he concluded the conversation. "If you ever get to Cleveland, look me up. That's Cleveland, Cleveland Ohio, Cleveland Ohio U.S.A."

With each pronouncement, Quinter thrust the cigar closer to the face of the nervous passenger, tossing the box in the man's lap. He then walked three or four remaining steps to the washroom, threw some water on his face, wiped it dry and quickly ran a comb through his hair before leaving the rest-room. The man was nowhere to be seen. Jennifer was pointing toward the front of the train. Quinter's face broke into an ugly grin as he returned to her seat.

"I couldn't figure out whether to hit the son of a bitch or not," he said, through his teeth, "I think he's the man who ran into me coming out of my office, but I'm not a hundred percent sure. We'll be alright. They're too many people for him to try anything. Although, I almost wish that he would. The odds are good that he and I have a score to settle."

Jennifer had been looking at Quinter as he talked. She had never seen Quinter display this kind of intensity, and the metamorphosis both worried and fascinated her.

"Are you O.K.?" she asked after several minutes.

"I'm fine now, but I came close to losing it a few minutes ago."

The train was now traveling through the valleys and passes of the Betic Mountains. The misting rain had stopped for some time, and occasionally, brilliant shafts of sunlight shone between the broken clouds. The views were breathtaking—enormous brown and red outcroppings of rugged rock that overlooked lush green valleys a thousand feet below on one side and immediately adjacent to flat land on the other, stretching toward level rolling brown hills. The view was accentuated by areas of intense color highlighted by the bright sun.

A Roman aqueduct built on four tiers of arches paralleled the track for a short distance, then took an angular course and receded from view behind a low rise. Off in the hills there was a little mountain village with white-stuccoed houses, and red-tiled roofs, connected by common walls, all of which were outlined in immaculate detail against the soft-toned foot-hill in the distance.

Quinter shifted in his seat. It had been over an hour since his encounter with the stocky man, and, uncharacteristically, he had been unable to decide on a course of action. He and Jennifer would undoubtedly be safe on the public train, but the real question was whether or not he should try to find the man and settle the matter. The approach of the conductor announcing their arrival in Malaga in twenty-five minutes distracted him, and he defaulted to inaction.

"Jenny," Quinter began," I don't think we should stay in Malaga tonight. Let's get a car and head up the coast. There are some wonderful little towns near Almuñécar. It'd give us an opportunity to put some time and distance between us and our friends. I know a car rental place in the center city that'll be happy to pick us up. The owner is a fellow named José Luis whom I met several years ago. His brother runs a real estate agency, so he may be a useful contact."

"O.K.," said Jennifer, "sounds reasonable to me."

As the train rounded a curve and began its gradual descent, the Mediterranean Sea came into view for the first time. Spread out on the coastal plain below was the brawny seaport of Malaga, surrounded by low mountains. The closest of these was red-gold in color, scarred by the timeless effect of wind and water erosion. The distant mountains stopped just short of the sea, and appeared more regular, taking on a purple cast. A few puffy white clouds dotted the sky.

In the brilliant sunshine, the sparkling blue sea was bordered by a strip of sandy brown sand. The vista was a wonderful blending of reds, golds, browns, infinite shades of blue and occasional patches of green.

What beautiful country, Jennifer thought.

"Lovely," said Quinter.

The train lurched to a stop at the Malaga station. The couple gathered their luggage, got off the train, and began walking down the platform in the direction of the station when Quinter stiffened.

"Jennifer!" he whispered under his breath, "look straight ahead, toward the front door of the next car."

The stocky man was walking toward the station. He appeared to be listening intently to a man with a thin moustache who was dressed in a light brown suit and carrying a small leather briefcase.

"It's our friend, and his companion is the same guy I saw watching us as we were leaving the Madrid airport, and, unless I'm mistaken, the one who followed us to the hotel."

Suddenly, a part of the puzzle made sense. There was a connection between the Cleveland and Madrid assaults. But what was the reason?

Keeping a good distance behind the men, who were immersed in intense conversation and apparently unconcerned with events around them, Quinter and Jennifer walked into the station. Although the station was crowded, Quinter had little trouble following the men as they walked to the front entrance.

He and Jennifer continued to follow them, discretely, through the main lobby and outside the station to a semi-circle where a number of cars and taxis were waiting. Quinter, squinting involuntarily in the bright sunshine, saw the men get into a long black limousine which pulled away from the station quickly. As the vehicle picked up speed, its red, black, and white fender flags unfurled to show three green stars.

"My god, Jennifer, that's an Iraqi diplomatic car."

SEATED IN A large wing chair in his Madrid hotel suite, Bordman was mentally recounting the events of the morning. Exactly on the stroke of 10:00, he, Tester, and Joel Johnson had been ushered into the ornate inner office of the Spanish Minister of Defense. Butler was asked to wait in the outside office.

The Minister and his Chief of Staff greeted the three Americans as if they were all old friends. After an exchange of pleasantries, the Spaniards advised them it would be in the best interests of everyone to speed up delivery of the weapons.

"The current political situation is less than stable," the Minister began, "and the government believes that the sooner the munitions are delivered and transported to the respective arsenals and out of public view, the better for the domestic peace."

"I agree," Bordman replied. "Picketers were at the airport yesterday morning, and I have no doubt there will be continued, and extensive, media coverage."

"We are prepared to be in position to accept the first shipment late Wednesday afternoon, as called for in the original delivery schedule," the Minister continued. "Can you make such a delivery?"

"I'm expecting a call from our man in Lisbon this afternoon giving final confirmation," Bordman responded, "but I have no reason to believe the timing cannot be met."

"There is, of course, the question of the consideration for the other venture," the Minister stated, smoothly.

"Yes, it's all here," Bordman said with a slight smile, gesturing toward the leather briefcase at the side of Tester's chair. "Korny, please give the consideration to the Minister."

Tester arose from his chair, briefcase in hand and walked around the Minister's desk, placing the briefcase in front of him. He unlatched the two clasps and opened the cover revealing numerous packets of one hundred dollar bills.

"Here it is, Sr. Minister, $500,000 in accordance with our agreement, the rest to follow upon completion of the transaction."

In a cursory inspection, the Minister riffed the edges of three of the packets, nodded his approval, closed the briefcase, and handed it to his Chief of Staff.

"Very well," he replied, "I will await your call of confirmation."

Bordman picked up the remote control from the top of the TV and began sifting through the channels. Finding nothing that interested him, he settled back in the comfortable chair to wait for a call from Jones. He glanced at his watch, noting it was quarter of two, and thinking that Jones would be calling in 15 minutes.

He closed his eyes and began smiling as he recalled his first meeting, just over three years ago, with Duane Johnson. As he did so, his smile broadened.

Having let word get out that he was interested in leaving government, Bordman had expected calls. Nonetheless he was surprised that one of the first was from the president and CEO of Nortex, inviting him to lunch in Washington at the prestigious Cosmos Club on Massachusetts Avenue.

Bordman was savvy enough to know that the invitation had undoubtedly been preceded by a careful screening of his views about a number of topics, in particular NATO, Spain and its government officials, general military build-up in the country, and the ongoing warfare between Iraq and Iran.

Bordman was sure Johnson knew that in his position with the State Department, he had developed a good working relationship with the Spanish Minister of Defense and many of the high-ranking officers in the Spanish military. However, when Bordman brought up that point in their initial phone conversation, Johnson feigned surprise.

"Well, isn't that interesting, David. As it happens," Johnson had said. "we're about to receive clearance from the Department of Defense for a large order to supply missiles, weapons, and other military hardware to Spain under the umbrella of NATO."

Deciding to employ candor, Bordman had replied, "Yes, I had heard something along those lines. Should be a nice chunk of business for your company."

"Indeed, but that's not the only reason I want to meet you. I think you and I should have lunch. Say, in Washington, tomorrow, noon, at the Cosmos Club?"

"That's good. See you then."

Bordman leaned back in his comfortable desk chair on the 5th floor, eastern corridor of *Foggy Bottom*, as Harry S Truman Building, the headquarters of the United States Department of State, is familiarly known. He had enjoyed his work as Assistant Under Secretary of State for Spanish Affairs. During his diplomatic career at State, he had made nine trips of various duration to the country, and had worked with and befriended a number of highly-placed government officials. But, pushing 41 and limited for several more years to making $56,000 because he'd reached the top of the GS 14 pay scale, Bordman was ready for new challenges, and more money.

The following day was one of Washington's spring specials—still too cool in the morning to walk outside without a coat, but so bright and clear it promised to be one of those lovely warm days on which it is almost impossible to do anything productive. Unbuttoning his raincoat Bordman walked up the curved driveway past the elaborately carved limestone planters, to the front entrance of the Cosmos Club. At exactly noon, he walked under the iron and glass marquee and through the door. He saw Johnson, whom he recognized from pictures in the financial pages, and the line drawing that had accompanied a recent profile of the industrialist in *The Wall Street Journal*, sitting in the vestibule. A smiling Johnson immediately stood up and started walking toward him.

"Hello David, Duane Johnson. Nice to meet you." Johnson said, extending his hand.

"Good to meet *you*, Mr. Johnson," Bordman said as they shook hands.

"Please, call me Duane. Check your coat over there, and let's go upstairs. We're having lunch in the Members' Dining room."

When Bordman returned, the two men walked up the carpeted staircase lined with an elegant wrought iron railing and center dividing handrail to the second floor, through the Long Gallery, and into the dining room where the maître d' greeted Johnson by name and escorted them to a good table.

After the waiter brought drink orders, Johnson turned to Bordman and said, "Tell me something about yourself." For the next 10 minutes Bordman recounted his college days, military service, and State Department experience.

"That's a nice resume, Dave," Johnson commented. "Pretty much as we researched it. Now, I hear you are ready to move on, and so I have a proposal for you to consider.

"I'm 67 and looking forward to a little less day-to-day involvement, but the company needs someone to pick up where I am going to leave off. Some folks at the company—and I—believe you could be that person. Some others have their doubts, given your lack of experience in the corporate, for-profit sector."

Johnson picked up his knife, turned the piece of silverware around in his hands, and then set it back down.

"But I have another reason, one of my own which I do not intend to share with the board. I see a great deal of myself in you. However, before you get all puffed up, that's not necessarily a compliment. What I mean is that I see certain ruthlessness. . ."

Johnson cut off the younger man before he could object. "And don't get coy with me, either. It doesn't suit you. We both know that the ethics office at State won't shed any tears over your leaving. They feel you cut too many corners too many times. Frankly, I have the same problem with one or two of my board members because of some rather, ah, unilateral decisions I made.

"And then there are your years at the CIA, which I noticed you didn't bother to mention. Again, there were problems. Am I correct?"

Bordman, sensing that for the moment his best weapon would be silence, nodded.

"Let's just say you got mixed reviews at the Company. . .

Deciding he'd waited long enough, Bordman interjected. "No, let's just say the dreamers at the top weren't sorry to see me go, but the realists, the few who know how the world works, were."

Pausing, Bordman took a small tan leather bound notebook out of his breast pocket, and flipped through a few pages.

"It seems to me, *Duane*, that you have a somewhat checkered past yourself, especially when it comes to certain long-running Middle Eastern and Central American conflicts in which the company seems to have made extraordinary and questionable profits off book."

Bordman closed the notebook and put it away. "There are times when a CIA background comes in quite handy."

At first, Johnson's brow furrowed, as if in anger, but then a slow smile of begrudging admiration crept across his face.

"David, I see we are going to get along just fine. Now let me be specific. I want you to be the point person on this deal with Spain. I'll make you Executive Vice President at a starting salary of $200,000, and your first job will be to close the deal with the Spaniards and oversee delivery of the material.

"This shouldn't be too much of a task. You already know the landscape, the players, and you won't be too upset if

116

things are not always done by the book or if they happen to get a little rough."

"That's probably true," replied Bordman, still seeking to recover his equilibrium. "Now," Johnson had continued, "there is another element that has to remain just between the two of us. Can you keep a confidence, David?"

Johnson had leaned over the table and was looking squarely into Bordman's eyes.

"I'm certain of it, Duane," said Bordman, staring right back.

"Good. I want you to know," Johnson added in a slightly quieter voice, "that I have a little side deal which you might call my special program for *personal* profit. It involves delivering some weapons to the Iranians so that they will have the ability to put a little more pressure on Saddam. I stand to make a whole lot of money—and if you can pull it off, there's a million in it for you."

"Jesus," Bordman replied, "we don't have any jurisdictional problems here, do we?"

"I don't think so, Dave. I know Senator James pretty well, a few contributions, you know. And Foggy Bottom has been sneaking missiles and arms to the Iranians for months. Not many folks even notice a slice missing from a cut loaf—much less get too upset about it."

"Sounds like you have it covered. You can count upon me, Duane."

"I'd hoped, no I'd thought I could. However, for appearance sake, there will need to be what you might call an apprenticeship, a demonstration of trust and loyalty, if you will. Should we give it a try?"

"Duane, I am honored, and almost speechless, and my answer is 'yes'."

"Good," said Johnson, and as the two men got up from the table, Johnson put his arm around Bordman's shoulder, and began walking him out toward the Long Gallery.

THE LOUD BUZZ of the ringing telephone interrupted Bordman's thoughts.

"Hello Dave, it's Ralph. I am pleased to report that the arrangements are progressing satisfactorily. The conversion and loading of the *Crescent* was completed early this morning and she set sail for Malaga just before noon. The Star will be underway in 24 hours. How did the meeting with the government go?"

"Exactly as planned." Bordman replied. "There will be no local interference, and indeed we can expect cooperation. I presume I can advise the Minister the original schedule will be met?"

"It's a 'go' all the way. Mother sends her regards, and I'll see you at the meeting Wednesday evening. Bye, Dave."

Bordman replaced the receiver and opened the door to an adjoining room. In one corner, Joel Johnson was slouched in an armchair, paging through the latest issue of "Cambio 16". In the adjacent corner, Tester was sitting behind a desk that held a small but powerful computer and a fax machine.

"Scramble a message to Mother." Bordman intoned. "It's a 'go.' Tell her the transaction is done. One bird's on the wing and the other leaves the nest tomorrow."

Tester placed the receiver in the fax cradle and began typing, looking up when he completed the message. In less than five minutes, the fax began to print a reply. Bordman walked over to the desk, and as the machine cycled to the end of the form, he ripped off the paper and read it to the group. "Message received. Good luck. Watch Quinter. Love, Mother." Bordman turned to Joel in a half-threatening, half-teasing manner, and said,

"Call Butler at room 329. Tell him to come over here and we'll all eat in the living room tonight. Then call room service and tell them to send up someone who speaks English. Do it, kid."

Joel, shaken, replied weakly, "Sure, Dave."

José Luis EXPERTLY negotiated the red Seát through the eastbound late Malaga rush hour traffic. He was delighted Quinter remembered him, and pleased he had picked his little agency.

"Would you like to drive, señor Quinter?"

"No thanks, José," Quinter replied," you're doing fine. But I would like to make a phone call when you can find a telephone."

"I know a place just past the Bull Ring, señor Quinter," José replied. "There it is now, señor."

José double-parked the Seát in front of a café. Quinter and Jennifer went inside, and Jennifer called the number Quinter had been given.

"David, this is Jennifer. Tom wants to speak with you."

"Why Jennifer, how good to hear from you," said Bordman. Jennifer handed the phone to Quinter.

"David, Tom here. We've had quite a time of it."

Quinter recounted the knife assault near the frog fountain, the incident on the train, and the departure of the two men in the Iraqi diplomatic vehicle.

Accepting the news without comment, Bordman said simply, "Tom, there's been a change of plans. We'll need the villa for a meeting Wednesday night. Also, make sure the farm is located just west of Malaga. Things are getting pretty hot here politically and time is short."

Something in Bordman's voice caught Quinter's attention. Bordman's lack of concern over the events Quinter had just related? His sense of urgency? But the bond of trust Quinter thought he still had with Bordman began to weaken as Quinter realized that Bordman knew more than he would tell.

He gathered his senses and responded confidently, "There should be no problem, Dave. I'll call you back at this number tomorrow at 2:00."

"You do that, Tom," replied Bordman. Quinter hung up.

BORDMAN STARED FIERCELY at his half-eaten dinner.

"The God damn Iraqis are onto him. They must have been bugging my phone *before* I went to Cleveland," he said under his breath.

"I'm sorry, Dave?" inquired Graham Butler.

"Oh, nothing," said Bordman, now underplaying his reaction, "Let's eat."

THE CLOCK ON the bureau read 9:30. Quinter walked over to the small balcony where Jennifer stood looking out across the lights of Almuñécar to the dark sea beyond. The night was clear but cool and over her shoulders Jennifer wore a red, yellow, and blue shawl she had purchased several hours earlier in the marketplace.

Quinter put his arm around her shoulder. For a while they said nothing, content to stand and watch the changing visual patterns, enjoying the cool breeze, and smelling the tangy salt air. Jennifer spoke first.

"Something happened when you talked with David today, didn't it," she said softly.

"Butler was right," replied Quinter, "Bordman and the others are involved in more than an approved sale of arms to a member of NATO. When I told Dave what happened to us, he seemed to expect we would have problems. Even worse, he gave no sign of caring, as long as I got him his damn property. David's changed, and I don't like it."

"Well, come on, honey," said Jennifer, turning to Quinter and brushing his hair back from his forehead with her fingers," we'll meet José's brother in the morning, find David his property, and leave these people to their scheme."

Quinter nodded, and they walked off the balcony into the room.

10

QUINTA DE LA TORRE

QUINTER WOKE, AND, SEEING JENNIFER was not next to him, sat upright in the bed until he saw, with relief, that she was sitting on the balcony. The morning sun was low in the sky to her left.

Below the balcony a curved terrace was bordered by a stone wall set with blue and gold ceramic tiles. A stone walk outlined by a single tier of red brick and a double row of red rose bushes ran from the terrace to the front door of the house. Between the walk and the wall a myriad of Mediterranean plants and shrubs, most in full bloom, provided cascades of color and shape.

Half a mile away, a white sand beach stretched to the west toward the village of Almuñécar. In the foreground a number of new apartment buildings were being completed. Beyond the construction were the lower houses and stores of the central city, the sparkling blue bay, and an outcropping of the low coastal mountains. From the center of the village, a smaller and more rugged peninsula jutted out into the flat sea in a series of humps. On the largest of these, a stone floor surrounded by a low wall had been constructed, and in the middle stood a white stone cross thirty feet high.

Antonio Luis, José's brother, had a thriving business, as evidenced by his incessantly ringing telephone. He greeted Jennifer and Quinter, and gestured for them to sit in the wicker chairs in front of his large oak desk that was littered with papers and real estate magazines. Antonio took call after call. Finally, at the conclusion of one discussion, Quinter, slightly vexed, reached over and placed his hand on the telephone.

"Antonio," he began slowly in a measured tone, "now is the time for us to visit the villa you told us about."

"A thousand pardons, Mr. Quinter," said Antonio in perfect English, "I did not mean to be rude. The telephone is so insistent. Come and I shall take you to Quinta de la Torre. Quinta is a beautiful villa and you will like it very much. But first let me show you La Torre."

The tower overlooked the small village of La Herradura. La Torre stood on the peak of the ridge of the peninsula from which there was a breathtaking unobstructed view of a long stretch of the Costa del Sol. To the east was the town of Almuñécar and to the west, La Herradura nestled in the center of a horseshoe-shaped bay.

Luis parked the car off the paved serpentine road in front of Quinta's garage. The group endured a stiff climb to reach the ridge and the tower. Quinter, wiping the perspiration from his forehead with the back of his hand, looked at Antonio Luis, who was directing Jennifer's attention toward a stone tower on an adjacent ridge some fifteen miles west of the village.

"That tower is an exact duplicate of the one behind us," he began. "The towers were used by the Moors to signal the approach of enemy and other ships many years ago. When a ship appeared on the horizon, a fire would be lit at the top of the tower. Once the smoke was seen, the sentinels in the next tower would light a fire to carry the message.

In this way, information could be conveyed up and down the coast, and many days of warning could be given."

Jennifer looked at the tower behind her. It was at least forty feet high and fifteen feet across at the base. The brown stone bricks had been expertly wedged together and cemented with a primitive but effective mortar. Narrow slits in the base showed the wall was at least eighteen inches thick.

"It must have taken an enormous amount of work to build these," Jennifer said.

"Many years," Antonio replied. "Shall we return to Quinta de la Torre? That means 'fifth from the Tower,' you understand."

The group started down the dirt path back toward the road 300 feet below. Torre Road serpentined down to the coast, two thousand feet below and a mile distant. Along the road there was an unending line of villas, each set upon a tier or retaining wall above the one below.

When they reached the villa, Antonio, using a strangely shaped triangle key, unlocked and pushed open the heavy wooden entrance door built through the nine-foot wall. A narrow stone walk led through rock gardens and beds of flowers and cacti grew in a curved path for about 100 feet down a steep decline to the rear of the house. In the center of the villa there was a courtyard with a fountain circled by five blossoming orange trees. The sweet smell of orange filled the courtyard and drifted through the four sets of open double glass doors, permeating the entire house.

Toward the sea, the courtyard joined a wide porch that extended for 50 feet across the entire front of the structure, overlooking the ocean and La Herradura. Several groups of chairs and glass-topped tables were arranged along the porch, below which was a hundred-foot swath of lush green grass that ran from side to side between the walls, ending at a tiered series of gardens stretching down the hill to the lower wall at the front of the grounds. A three-foot chain link fence tipped by razor wire topped the lower wall. Quinta was indeed well-fortified.

They walked through the modern kitchen, down three steps to the living room, through another set of double glass doors, and across the patio to the front porch.

"Where did you learn English, Antonio?" Quinter asked, as the three sat down at one of the tables.

"My father was in the export business," Antonio replied, "and his affairs required him to travel to America. I went with him a number of times, and when he asked me if I would like to continue my schooling in America, I accepted. I am a graduate of the City College of New York."

Antonio pulled some papers from an envelope.

"That explains why your English is so good." said Quinter. "Your parents are Spanish?"

"My father is, but my mother is Iraqi. In fact I stayed with her relatives when I was in school in New York. So, do you think you will take Quinta de la Torre?" Antonio inquired.

"Yes," answered Quinter. "It's just fine."

"It's lovely," said Jennifer, "and all those flowers, and cacti, and strangely-shaped palm trees are exquisite."

"O.K.," continued Antonio," You said one month? "Here is your receipt for 4000 pesetas, one-half month's rent. The balance will be due in two weeks."

Quinter took four one thousand peseta notes from his breast pocket wallet, and offered them to Antonio. "I'll bet you have some pretty strong feelings about the Iran-Iraq fighting."

Antonio winced ever so slightly.

"Many differences exist between the two countries, Mr. Quinter. Arguments can be made for both peoples, but much hot blood flows, and many have died."

Quinter noted that his question had been evaded.

Here is the key, Mr. Quinter, I know you will enjoy your stay. The sunsets are beautiful. Innocencia will be along to prepare lunch. She will shop for you if you would like. She leaves at two o'clock and will be back in the morning to fix breakfast and tidy up. I'll be going now. Good-bye señorita. Good-bye Mr. Quinter. You know where to find me." Antonio rose from the chair, extended his hand in turn to Jennifer and Quinter, and departed.

QUINTER LAY ON his back looking up at the cathedral ceiling and wooden beams that spanned the bedroom. He felt a vague sense of unease as he slipped out from under the single sheet that covered him and Jennifer and walked the short distance to the front window. The light of the full moon cast long, eerie shadows over the countryside, alternatively appearing and disappearing when puffy clouds blocked the light. The breeze began to quicken and the trees and plants swayed back and forth causing the shadows to meld and blur in a shifting collage.

Looking out toward the sea, he could make out the distinct form of waves, now and then breaking into an occasional whitecap. The sound of the wind went up and down the scale as it blew through the pine trees.

Quinter looked at his watch in the moonlight. 4:30. His mind wandered to earlier in the evening when he and Jennifer sat on the porch watching the sun set. As it descended to the horizon it deepened in color and when the leading edge of the deep orange ball touched the point where sea met sky, Jennifer said she imagined she could feel the earth turn. Then it was gone, and daylight turned to twilight in the afterglow.

A barely audible click of metal against stone interrupted his reverie. Still naked, and with his adrenaline cresting,

Quinter moved out into the hallway. As he entered the back bedroom, his right shin struck a small footstool. Despite the excruciating pain, he choked down all sound. He crouched low by the window in time to see a glint of curved metal near the back wall.

Transfixed, he heard the sound of low voices, and saw a dark figure appear at the top of the wall. He watched as the figure squatted on the wall, and then, in one fluid motion, dropped to the ground, next to another form.

"Jesus!" he murmured as he hurriedly retraced his steps to the front room and clambered across the bed to where Jennifer lay. "Jennifer, Jennifer! Wake up! We have visitors! Jennifer, wake up, damn it!" he whispered urgently while shaking her shoulders.

"What is it, Tom, what's happening?"

"Two people just climbed over the wall and I think at least one of them has a scimitar! Get dressed, no lights!" Quinter had already pulled on his trousers and was buckling his belt. "Just put on anything, and some shoes. These people mean harm."

Quinter tied his shoes feverishly, opened the closet door and pulled the shoulder holster from the hook. He snapped open the holster, grabbed one of the ammunition pockets and, retrieving the 7.65 mm Mauser, slammed home the magazine.

His mind was racing. He had to make a stand. Where? There was not much time. The den just before it widened out into the living room. He would have the stone fireplace at his back, and no windows to worry about. But to maintain his advantage, he had to get past the glass patio doors before his adversaries got to the front porch. From the den, he could cover the rear entrance as well, since they would have to pass in front of him on their way to the stairs. "Jenny, we're going to the den."

Quinter grabbed Jennifer's hand and pulled her toward the door. Quickly, they moved across the landing and down the double flight of steps. They reached the first floor, where moonlight flooded the living room.

Pausing briefly to assess the situation, Quinter then moved rapidly and stealthily across the living room, around the twin opposing sofas to the den. He motioned to Jennifer to crouch behind a small but solid table. Taking a poker from the stand of fire tools, he handed the instrument to her without a word, and then walked several steps to a large overstuffed chair and turned it around so that the rear faced the fireplace in the back wall of the den.

As he moved the chair back several feet, Quinter noticed the track lighting which served to illuminate several works of art along the hallway corridor. At the same time a cloud passing in front of the moon cast the entire area in darkness. Instinctively, Quinter raced to the lights, bending one to the left toward the kitchen and rear door, another to the right toward the foot of the stairs, and a third in the direction of the patio. He adjusted the chair on his way back so that it was closer to the wall with the back just on the living room side of the switch.

"And now, Jenny, we will find out if the hunters shall become the hunted. Use the poker if you have to—just don't hit me," he said with a weak grin.

"I'm scared."

"I'm scared too, Jenny, but these bastards are going to get more than they bargained for."

The cloud passed from the moon and again the area was filled with light. *Good,* Quinter thought, *If this keeps up, there's no way we can miss them.* He pulled back the slide of the Mauser, cocking the weapon, and in the relative darkness they waited, silent and motionless.

The breeze, which had become wind, spread in gusts from the ocean to the shore up the mountain through the trees and toward the tower. As it blew across the chimney of the villa, it caused a rising and lowering moan-like sound. The porch, patio, and living room were alternatively immersed in light and semi-darkness as the clouds flew by the moon.

Time passed. They heard nothing.

"Damn," said Quinter, half to himself, "where are they? Do you hear anything Jenny?"

"Nothing," she whispered, "Maybe they decided not to make the attempt."

"Not a chance." replied Quinter softly, "They've come too far already."

His sentence was interrupted by a scratching noise on one of the patio doors as the wind bent the branch of an orange tree so that it made contact with the glass in a scraping sound. Quinter tensed reflexively and then relaxed. More time passed, and the chimney moaned.

The instant they appeared from behind the column separating the patio from the porch, Quinter saw the two figures, silhouetted in the moonlight. One stepped forward, and laid a small bag on the tile floor outside of the glass. He removed a tool, attached it to the glass near the lock, and began to scratch a full circle. Quinter crouched low behind the chair so that he was able see the area with just his right eye.

"Not a sound, Jenny," he whispered, his gut taut with anticipation.

Shortly, the glass was removed, and after reaching through the circle and unlocking the door, the two figures moved quickly across the patio. Again, the taller silhouette positioned the tool on the glass door and scribed a circle.

130

The glass oval made a soft pop as it broke free from the pane, and a hand appeared on the living room side of the door, expertly finding the lock.

In a moment, Jennifer heard the lock click as the bolt was withdrawn, and the door opened slowly. Perspiration of fear trickled between her breasts and dripped on the inside of the tee shirt she had pulled on so hastily just moments ago.

The doors seemed to stick for a brief moment, and then Quinter heard the low grunt of measured exertion as the man applied strength.

Suddenly both men, speaking softly in a strange language, were in the living room, not twenty feet away.

Quinter inched his hand higher on the track light switch.

Their conversation finished, the men began moving toward the stairs as the moonlight dimmed in the room. With the switch in his left hand and the Mauser in his right, Quinter threw the switch and yelled at the top of his voice, "Don't move you bastards or you're fuckin' dead."

The bright lights from the track light, the loud sound of a human voice behind them, and the complete surprise of the attack disoriented the assailants. Yet the first man whirled around, hurling a flashing scimitar in Quinter's direction. At that identical second, Quinter fired two shots, the first buried itself in the man's skull just below his left eye and the second ripped into his throat. As he fell heavily to the floor, a spurting arc of blood splattered on the face of his bewildered conspirator.

The butt of the flying scimitar grazed the left side of Quinter's head, and he dropped to his knees, his head reeling. The blade sped past him and lodged in a wooden beam next to the fireplace. Dazed, Quinter, hearing Jennifer call his name just as the second man gave his guttural battle screech, raised his head to see the attacker rushing toward him from ten feet away, his scimitar held high over his head.

Jennifer, sensing that Quinter would not be able to recover in time to defend himself, intuitively timed her attack. When the man was five feet from Quinter, screaming, and about to bring the great knife down, Jennifer moved in from the side. With both hands and all her strength, she brought the poker down in a sickening thud on the left side of the attacker's head.

The force of the blow knocked him to the tile floor, and blood immediately began to flow from his crushed skull. Rising unsteadily to his feet, Quinter steadied himself against the wall.

"Good God, Jenny," he stammered, I think . . . I never could have . . . you saved my life."

Jennifer stood facing him. The poker was still in her right hand pointing downward. Pieces of flesh and blood were attached to the hook at the end.

"Is he dead?" she asked in an almost child-like voice.

Quinter, regaining his senses, scarcely felt the pain from the blow to his head. He took two steps, the second one over the dislodged scimitar, then bent over the fallen body, and with both hands rolled the man on his back searching first for life and then for personal items. He found nothing.

"Jesus, it's the man we saw on the train. He's dead."

Jennifer looked hard at the stocky man, his thick black hair now matted with fresh red blood still flowing from the open head wound. Her memory flashed to when she had surprised the intruder in the office in Cleveland. Then, she said sharply,

"It's the same son of a bitch who struck me in our office."

Jennifer began to comprehend the horror that surrounded them. As her mind cleared she looked down at the poker in her right hand. She let the instrument slip from her hand, and it clanged as it fell against the tiles.

132

"I don't remember ever seeing this one," Quinter called out to her from across the room. "There's no identification, but whoever he is, he's not very pretty now."

Jennifer forced herself to look at the man's distorted face and neck. Nausea gripped her as she saw the ooze of his body fluids and the jagged edges of his torn flesh.

After completing his inspection, Quinter walked back to Jennifer, and they held each other for several minutes without speaking.

"Are you O.K.?" asked Quinter softly.

"I'm fine," said Jennifer with a sense of confidence that surprised her, "but look at your poor head."

Quinter grunted.

"I suppose we should call the police," she suggested.

"I think not," replied Quinter striding toward the living room telephone, "but I have a better idea." Quinter punched in the numbers from memory. The phone rang ten times before Bordman answered with a sleepy, "Yes."

"Bordman, this is Quinter. What the hell is going on?"

11

THE FARM

DAWN BROKE AS THE RED Seát headed south away from the coast and Quinta de la Torre toward National Route E-26, the highway to Malaga. The sky was gray and a fine mist permeated the air. Jennifer reclined her seat and was resting with her head back and her eyes closed, exhausted, apparently asleep. Quinter studied her. *What would I have done without her?* he wondered. *One thing's certain, I wouldn't be sitting here now. Man, she's got real guts. And a great sense of timing! Praise be for that. . .* Her physical proximity gave him a sense of comfort.

He was, however, decidedly uncomfortable with the plan and instructions he'd just received. Bordman had told him to proceed to Malaga as originally scheduled, and find the farm since the first shipment of NATO weapons would be arriving at the port in the afternoon. Bordman said "my people. . ." would dispose of the bodies.

Quinter, questioning Bordman's timing, told him the maid, Innocencia, would come to the villa in just a few hours.

But Bordman assured him everything would be accomplished in sufficient time, reminding him that Nortex needed the villa for an important meeting in the evening. He would see that everything was in order and "cleaned up".

Quinter had feigned reassurance, but he felt no trust, and wondered whether he had unwittingly given Bordman and Nortex a major advantage.

Bordman had said that if they wished, Quinter and Jennifer could consider their work complete, and that a Nortex jet could meet them at the Malaga airport whenever they wanted. Quinter, knowing that the job was definitely unfinished and now suspicious of Bordman's intentions, declined.

The rhythmic slap of the windshield wipers brought Quinter's attention back to the highway, and he steered the Seát to the left just in time to prevent the right wheels from leaving the roadway and entering the berm. The slight lurch of the vehicle jostled Jennifer, and she opened her eyes as they passed a sign announcing Nerja.

"Aren't the Caves located near here, Tom? I've heard they're amazing."

"Yes," answered Quinter, "but that's for another day, unfortunately. Grab my jacket from the rear seat and check for a pack of matches in the left side pocket."

"I have them," she replied, "Don't tell me you're going to smoke one of those horrible Spanish cigars."

"I may in a few minutes," he returned, "but there should be the name of a hotel in Almuñécar listed on the front. If we should ever get separated, we will meet there. Register under your mother's maiden name. Rose, isn't it? I'll register under my mother's, Andros. By the way, copy Jeff Downing's telephone number. I wrote it on one of my cards in my wallet, which should be in the breast pocket."

Jennifer wrote the number inside the cover of the matchbook, making a mental note that the hotel was named La Regencia.

"I suspect this may well be an unnecessary precaution, but . . ." Quinter's voice trailed off.

"Understood." Jennifer finished.

Quinter looked at his watch. It was a little after 7:00 o'clock in the morning. The sky was brighter now but still overcast and mist partially obscured the view of the highway.

Low scud clouds hanging below the high overcast layer rolled in from the sea brushing the foothills of the coastal mountains and turning them a dull brown-gray. From time to time the higher peaks would recede from view behind the gray mist only to reappear a minute or so later. The sea breeze was steady, the sea a deep undulating blue-green.

Quinter followed the highway toward the center of the city as its name changed to Paseo Sancha, then Avenida de Pries, then Paseo Reding as it passed by the bull ring, and then Paseo del Parque as it continued west of the city paralleling the seaport on the left.

Paseo del Parque was bordered by a wide pedestrian walkway showing a gray background with red and blue linear patterns of no discernible order. On either side, the walkway was lined with rows of lush palm trees twenty-five feet high. Behind the palms the branches of a row of larger, more widely-spaced trees gave the illusion of a towering arch.

When they arrived at the Plaza Quiepo Llano at the foot of the broad Avenida de General Alissimo, Quinter pulled up in front of a small café.

"We have some time to kill, so let's get something to eat," he said.

Quinter and Jennifer lingered for more than an hour over croissants and café con leche. From their table next to the front window they looked outside as increasing numbers of people filled the sidewalk. After nine o'clock, Jennifer began placing calls to real estate agents she selected at random from the telephone book.

Each time she would inquire whether the agent knew of a farm for rent located west of the city, out N-340 toward the airport or out MA-401 or MA-405 toward Campanillas. At the fourth call, the agent who answered said he did have such a place about two kilometers east of Campanillas. He would show it to her at 11:30. Jennifer accepted immediately.

"Mission accomplished," she said to Quinter with a feeling of self-satisfaction.

"Well done," he replied with a grin. "Now try this one."

He handed her the card with Bordman's Madrid number on it, again relieved not to deal with the Spanish long distance telephone system.

Jennifer struggled with the bureaucracy for several minutes, and when the line began to ring, handed the phone to Quinter. Shortly, a voice answered.

"Hello."

Quinter recognized the voice immediately.

"Graham. This is Tom Quinter."

After a brief moment, Quinter heard the "Whew" of surprise followed by, "Tom, you've been a busy boy. Got everyone here all uptight. Are you and Jennifer all right?"

"As of the moment, yes, but we had a nasty time. Where's Bordman?"

"He took the some Iranians to Barajas Airport to make final arrangements for the flight, and lord knows what else. I'm to meet them there at one o'clock for a helicopter flight directly to La Herradura. I think the final destination is Quinta de la Torre."

138

"That's the villa, Graham. Jenny and I spent the night there, or at least part of the night. We were stalked by some Iraqi thugs."

"Iraqi!" questioned Butler," You said Iraqi?"

"That's right. Didn't Bordman tell you? At least one of those bastards had been tracking us on and off all the way from Cleveland."

"Bordman doesn't tell me much these days, Tom, but. . . Hey! Wait a minute. Just before I came on board last year there was a big flap about a possible breach of security in Bordman's office involving his phones and his interoffice communication system. That could be your Iraqi-Cleveland connection. They've known that Nortex has been supplying the Iranians for a while"

"That may be it, Graham," said Quinter slowly. "But you were saying?"

"Oh, right. I hear there's a big meeting with some Iranian heavy hitters tonight at this Quinta place. And from the involvement of Jones and the Energia Division, I'm betting it has something to do with oil. In fact, one of our tankers is due to arrive in the port of Malaga today. A ship called the *Crescent*."

"Iranians, huh? Now I wonder what's that all about?" He was only half-surprised when he heard Butler's response.

"I don't know, Tom, but be careful. My guess is that you're not safe, that someone probably is or will be after you. No hard evidence. Just gut instinct, but the kind I trust a lot. You can reach me at the villa in La Herradura, Quinta, tonight and tomorrow."

"The telephone number is . . ."

Quinter interrupted," I have it."

"Alright," said Butler. "Take care, my friend."

"Bye, Graham. Thanks for the info and appreciate the thought. But don't you worry about the cat gettin' fat or the mule goin' blind," he replied leaving Butler chuckling at another of his step father's favorite expressions.

Jennifer, who could tell that Quinter was both troubled and confused, said nothing, and they walked hand in hand back to the table and the cooling café con leche. Rubbing the sides of his face and forehead with his hands, Quinter sat down and then he spoke slowly to her, "We may be pawns in a Middle-Eastern war in which Nortex is manipulating the game. But what I don't yet know is why or how. But I think we need to find out. Let's pay our bill and get out of here."

Quinter and Jennifer walked across the Plaza Queipo Llano and started up the Paseo del Parque in the direction of a group of horse-drawn carriages. The light mist had stopped, but the clouds were thicker and the sky darker. Arriving at the place where the drivers gathered, they were besieged with solicitations. At first, Quinter raised his hand in a show of refusal, but on second thought, and after a nudge from Jennifer, he asked her to find out if anyone made the rounds of the port.

"The lead driver says he has a fine tour of the port," Jennifer said with the first smile Quinter had seen in a while.

"Tell him 'yes,' Jenny."

The driver escorted them to his carriage, and they climbed in and seated themselves on its bright red leather seats.

The vehicle had been beautifully maintained. The spokes of all four wheels were freshly painted a bright yellow-orange to match the drawbars. The black fenders formed of bent wood, swooped down in a graceful curve and at their lowest point became the running board. A brass lantern, with four square glass panes, was bolted to a tubular black metal stem on each of the front fenders, and a black leather three-quarter roof was drawn over the passenger seat. At the front, the driver sat on a red leather box seat without a back. The well-oiled black reins looked supple.

The carriage was drawn by a small white mare named Annabel, young, but strong and obviously well-trained. Pablo, the driver, short and slender, was tanned and wrinkled from years of exposure to the tropical sun. As Annabel lurched the carriage into motion, Quinter said, "Ask him to describe the port as we go, Jenny. You know, where the cargo ships off-load, where the oil tankers dock, where the warehouses are located . . ."

WHEN GRAHAM BUTLER arrived shortly before 1:00 o'clock, the private aviation gate at Barajas airport was practically empty. In halting Spanish he asked the attendant behind the desk whether she had met any people from Nortex, a Mr. Bordman or a Mr. Jones. The woman replied, in perfect English, that she had just come on duty a few minutes before he arrived and had not yet seen anyone.

His hands folded across his stomach, Butler sat on one of the benches in the waiting area and gazed through the wide glass windows at the rows of aircraft parked on the tarmac. He could see the painted landing circles where the helicopter pilots brought their craft to rest.

Mentally, he replayed the events of the last several days, and as he did so he began to frown. The attacks on Quinter and Jennifer were deeply disturbing, and left him with a growing feeling of dread, especially since he was obviously being excluded from planning and decision-making.

Butler, who had vast experience in security procedures, knew both from his background and his education that a security apparatus could not be effective unless there was a clear understanding of the elements that should be protected. He also knew from experience that while no security officer needed to participate in the formulation of specific political or economic decisions, his duties did require that he have input into the methods selected for implementing those decisions.

A little after one o'clock, the Nortex Apache Commuter helicopter appeared from behind the private aviation terminal, and the pilot guided the machine expertly to a gentle landing in the middle of the nearest circle. Before the rotor had come to a complete stop, the door, which doubled as entrance steps, swung down.

Cornelius Testor, followed by Ralph Jones, three men dressed in white robes and headdresses of various colors, and Dave Bordman descended the four steps. Butler walked over to the front of the waiting area to greet them.

"Good afternoon, gentlemen," Butler began easily, masking his irritation at having once again been left out.

"Hello Graham," replied Bordman. "I'd like to introduce you to Mr. Agajun, Mr. Maziar, and Mr. Mojtaba. Mr. Agajun and Mr. Maziar will be riding south with us today, and you may treat them as one of us. Mr. Mojtaba needs to catch a flight from the main terminal. Would you please escort him? We'll get started when you return."

"Very good," answered Butler. "This way, sir."

The two men left the group and walked out into the gray Madrid drizzle.

"What time is your flight, sir?" Butler asked his robed companion as they reached the main sidewalk and started toward the terminal.

"I have a 2:45 flight to Teheran, so we have ample time." Mojtaba replied with a British accent.

"Thank you, sir," Butler replied formally.

PARES GONZALEZ, THE self-proclaimed "Realty man who cares about you and your family" stood on the front porch of the

142

farmhouse straddling a broken floor board. His left hand was on his hip, and he was gesturing with the other toward the grove of olive trees.

"Aren't they lovely, and just look at those fields. Not another house for half a kilometer. Wonderful privacy. The owner died six months ago," he said dramatically.

"How much?" asked Quinter.

"Only 5000 pesetas a month. A real bargain," said Gonzales. Quinter studied the house. The white alabaster had become a dirty brown, and was both cracked and absent in numerous places. The roof was missing a number of tiles and the black paint on the framing around the door and windows was crazed and cracked. One of the steps leading from the porch to the ground was missing an entire board.

"A real bargain," repeated Quinter, as he took five one-thousand peseta notes from his wallet, "We'll take it. You have the key?"

"You won't need one, Mister Quinter," answered Gonzalez, but you can bolt the doors from the inside, and the windows are small. You'll be perfectly safe. No one ever comes around here anyway. The water runs. The telephone works. And look at the rows of almond trees, and those fig trees. In a perfect line. Magnificent! And what better view of the ocean could you expect? You can be seaside in less than twenty minutes."

"Sold," said Quinter, handing Gonzalez the five bills.

"Gracias, señor. You will not be sorry," said the realtor giving Quinter the receipt, and bowing in a mock show of respect. "I'll be going now. Adios."

"Well, Jenny," said Quinter with a broad grin on his face as they watched Gonzalez shuffle happily down the stone walk toward the gravel driveway, "it's all ours."

"How romantic!" Jennifer sighed, as if allowing herself to be caught up in the game.

Quinter followed Gonzalez's old brown Citroën with his eyes as it disappeared down the highway leaving a trail of oil smoke. He scanned the sea, noting several ships of varying sizes, and the largest, a tanker.

"Jenny, look at that ship. I think that's our baby. I'll get the binoculars."

Quinter walked to the parked Seát and took the binoculars from the glove compartment. Flipping the adjusting switch to long range, he brought the vessel into focus. Even from this distance, the gold Nortex insignia on the smokestack was clear as were members of the crew standing along the railing.

He guided the field of vision forward toward the bow, searching for the name and saw that the vessel was indeed the *Crescent*. Below the name, the red plimsel line was painted and from the markings, the vessel appeared to be slightly over half-full. Quinter handed the binoculars to Jennifer who trained them on the ship.

"What's happening?" she asked.

"Hard to say," answered Quinter. "Nortex is supposed to be making the first delivery of NATO weapons," he continued, "but I'm not quite sure how that could be done off this ship."

As if by a pre-arranged signal, a wave of fatigue flowed over Quinter,

"Jenny, I'm going to rest for a while. I think this will be a long evening."

Jenny looked at Quinter and saw black circles under his eyes.

"I'm tired too." Then, in a burst of emotion, she began crying uncontrollably. "Tom . . . Tom, did I really kill a person?"

"Yes you did." replied Quinter, "but you had no choice."

Their heads down and their arms interlocked, they set out toward the farmhouse.

144

12

THE CRESCENT

T HE PILOT HOVERED THE APACHE helicopter at the edge of
the sea just south of the Tower and below the overcast.
"I think I can put her down just beyond the tower on
the hilltop, Sir. According to the directions you gave me, we
ought to be close to this Quinta de la Torre. Probably one of
those villas just below the crest of the hill. La Herradura is
to the left. Almuñécar is just off to the right. Shall I take her
down, Sir?"

"Of course," said Bordman, quickly finishing his drink,
"Look out for wind shears."

Although there was no precipitation and the coastal wind
was blowing more steadily than it had all day, the heavy cloud
deck gave no sign of breaking up. The dark sea was lightened
by relentless white-capped surf that drove its way to the shore
pounding onto the darker wet sand of the beach.

As the Apache neared the cliffs and outcroppings of the
coastal mountains, the craft began to rise and descend irreg-
ularly in the varying air currents. The aircraft passed over

the Tower at a hundred feet and the pilot skillfully entered a power descent toward the flat brown earth just beyond, adjusting the throttle to counter the changing wind. At touchdown, he chopped the power and dumped the lift from the rotor.

"Bravo!" exclaimed Bordman, turning to his robed guests who appeared shaken and uneasy. "That was a magnificent performance, right?"

"Indeed," replied Mr. Agajun, composing himself.

Ralph Jones tightened his tie and wiped the perspiration from his forehead.

"Quinta de la Torre. That means 'fifth from the tower.' By my count, one, two, three, four, and five, it ought to be that house."

Jones had been marking off villas with his forefinger, and at his count of five, extended his right arm fully pointing toward Quinta de la Torre. "I think we have visitors. There's a van and three cars," Jones continued.

"I had the black Mercedes and the Volkswagen dropped off for our use. The van must belong to the caterers," added Bordman.

"And the new Citroën is ours," said Mr. Maziar.

The group left the craft, and started walking down the path toward the road and the villa, Bordman leading. When they neared the villa, a large, muscular heavy-set man in loose pantaloons appeared in front of the entrance, his arms folded across his chest. Mr. Maziar strode forward and they embraced on both cheeks in the Iranian custom.

"This is Abdullah, my protector," he stated, proudly.

The men passed through the door in single file. As he passed by the powerful man, Butler nodded, and looking Abdullah straight in the eye, casually said, "Howdy Bub." Abdullah grunted.

146

The group followed the curved path winding among the back gardens down to the rear entrance and into the kitchen where three men in chefs' toques were busily preparing culinary delicacies. The group walked out of the kitchen into the hallway, past the artwork illuminated by the track lights, down the steps, and across the red tile floor to the living room.

Nodding to Mr. Agajun and Mr. Maziar, Bordman said, "Have a seat gentleman. Ralph, ask the waiter to take drink orders."

Jones disappeared and in a moment returned with a waiter dressed in black tie and white gloves. Meanwhile, the men had seated themselves on the opposing sofas. A fire crackling in the stone fireplace across the room in the den cast a warm, flickering light throughout the two rooms.

When the waiter brought the drinks, Bordman toasted, "Here's to a job well done, and to a second job that will soon be well done," and the men laughed heartily.

Bordman turned to Butler and said, "Graham, I'd like you to skip desert and go to Malaga after dinner. Our guests have expressed an interest in seeing our ship, and we're going to give them the cook's tour. I want you to make sure all necessary security arrangements have been put in place. I don't have much faith in these local Spanish waterfront cops."

"Sure, Mr. Bordman," replied Butler.

Dinner, a sumptuous traditional Spanish style meal, was served in the dining room. A large silver plate piled high with shrimp, crab meat, oysters, clams and octopus had been placed in the center of the table on a white lace tablecloth.

After the appetizer, the chefs ceremoniously carried platters of roast lamb and trout to the table. Additional plates of asparagus, rice with chunks of lobster meat, and fresh fruit appeared, and the men settled down to serious eating. When desert, an assortment of cheeses, was served, Butler, as ordered, excused himself.

"Take the green Volkswagen," said Bordman. "Key's under the driver's seat. The *Crescent*'s at dock Seventeen West. We'll leave here in about an hour."

"Certainly, Mr. Bordman," responded Butler. "I'll be on top of everything by the time you arrive."

"Ask for Sergeant Dellanzo. He's in charge."

"Dellanzo. Yes Sir."

Butler started toward the kitchen and the rear entrance. As he walked up the curved path leading up to the back wall and Torre Road, he noticed that the wind had become a fresh breeze. The day was cooling, and he was lightly dressed.

If I'm going to be wandering around the docks tonight, I'd better get a jacket, he mused, reversing his path and starting back to the villa. He passed by the rear entrance to the kitchen and along the back of the house to the side entrance and his first floor bedroom. He walked up the four stone steps, opened the door, and proceeded down the hall until he reached his bedroom door.

As he entered his room, Butler could hear laughter coming from the living room. He took his windbreaker from the closet, and slipped it over his head.

As he paused to close the door on the way out, he heard Bordman say, softly but distinctly, "Mother and I think we have some personnel problems that need to be resolved."

"You mean your old friend and the woman?" queried Mr. Maziar.

"Yes," continued Bordman, "unfortunately, they are in a position to undermine our entire deal. Given all that's happened, I don't think Quinter will stop until he knows what's going on, and then he might do something foolish. I've given this a lot of thought and I'm afraid we have no option but to eliminate them—that is, if the Iraqis don't get them first."

Pushing his headdress back off his right shoulder with his left hand, Mr. Maziar said, "We have people who are skilled in these matters . . ."

Butler's face flushed and the hair on the back of his neck stood up as he waited motionless in the hallway, stunned by Bordman's words.

"And then, there's the question of your security man," continued Mr. Maziar smoothing his thin moustache with his finger. "I think he too presents a risk.

"He's just a dumb cop," said Bordman, "and he's ours."

"Abdullah despises him, as he does all police," said Maziar, "and would very much like the assignment of eliminating him."

"No sense in complicating matters," said Bordman. "He's bought and paid for, and he could be useful. We'll leave him alone for the time being. He doesn't know anything anyway. I made sure of that."

"Of course," replied Maziar as a wicked smile spread across his mouth, "but a time may come . . . and Abdullah . . ."

"It is settled," said Bordman, his blue eyes narrowed into a squint. "For now, just Quinter and the woman." A shaken Butler moved carefully and silently down the hallway to the side door. *"Those bastards!"* he murmured. And then softly to himself, *I think we shall have something to say about this.*

He returned along the tile walkway at the rear of the villa and up the path to the wooden door. He opened the door and Abdullah was sitting on the fender of the Volkswagen. "Abdullah, you son of a bitch, need your seat," he said with a smile to the huge Iranian who glared at him even though he did not understand a word.

Butler climbed into the driver's seat and started the engine, but Abdullah remained on the fender, his back to the windshield. When the man still did not move, Butler placed the car in gear and started moving down the road. After a few feet, the man pushed himself off the fender with one hand, yelling and shaking his fist.

"The same to you, Bub," Butler yelled back as the figure receded in the distance. *Yes*, he thought, *all in good time.*

QUINTER AWOKE IN the early evening, his arm around Jennifer. He entered the bathroom and began to splash cool water over his face. He inspected himself in the mirror. His blond hair stuck out in several places, thanks to the uncomfortable mattress.

Jennifer appeared behind him and—as her reflection also showed in the mirror—she rubbed her eyes. "What are you thinking, my love," she said tenderly.

"I am going to board the ship. Security will tight," he replied. "But I think a lot of questions will be answered."

SERGEANT DELLANZO WAS tired. He sat in the guardhouse at the entrance gate to Seventeen West, his feet up on the small desk, sipping his fourth cup of coffee. The cool brown liquid tasted terrible, but he continued to sip almost as much for lack of anything else to do as to keep from falling asleep. Patrolman Dunsos was making the rounds of the huge open black-topped storage area and the warehouse adjoining dock Seventeen West, and it would be another ten minutes before he returned.

The storage area had sections filled with stacked crates of various sizes off-loaded from the Crescent that was now docked parallel to the warehouse. Earlier, Dunsos had watched with some surprise when the crates began to follow one another in single file down the conveyor lines. Each one had the letters N A T and O spray-painted in black on the top and some sort of military identification coding was painted on the side.

He was also surprised to see standard wooden shipping crates coming off a ship that was so obviously built to carry bulk liquid. He knew the crates were heavy because the engines of the forklifts had labored during the stacking process, giving off clouds of black smoke.

Four small mountains of crates were set in the shape of a diamond and each was covered with tarpaulins, which were then weighted down on the edges with old tires attached to the canvas by ropes. The entire area was bathed in the harsh yellow glare of the sodium vapor lights that lined the chain link fence around the perimeter of the yard.

A HALF A MILE distant, from the entrance guardhouse, Quinter studied the scene from the driver's seat of the parked Seát. It was an intriguing problem. He waited while the guards made their rounds and timed them at intervals of 30 minutes, which, he figured should give him ample time—but first he had to slip in unseen.

Once he reached the point of the diamond he could move along it to the side of the warehouse, where the mountains would give him good cover from the view of the guardhouse. However, he would have to cross thirty yards of brilliantly illuminated open space during which time he'd be clearly visible from the guard station.

"Jenny, hand me the bag on the back seat, will you? I've got to put one of those lights out."

Quinter unzipped the bag, took out the silencer, and screwed the tubular metal onto the barrel of the Mauser.

"Honey," Quinter continued, pointing to his left and across the street, "I'm going to shoot out that near light from a position close to the corner of that old building. You stay here, in the car, and keep down. If anyone comes down the road, flash the lights. As soon as the light goes out, I expect the guards will investigate. So, regardless of who comes, keep the car lights off once the light is dead. Oh, and wish me luck."

"Be careful," she said pulling his head toward her and kissing him.

"I'll do my best," he said opening the car door.

Jennifer tracked Quinter as he crossed the street and began to work from tree to tree toward Seventeen West. She was relieved to see that his black sweater and dark jeans melded easily into the shadows. *I hope he's O.K.,* she thought anxiously. *I really love this guy so much.* Her attention was drawn to the rear view mirror by the lights of an approaching west-bound vehicle coming up the grade.

Reaching the corner of the last building before the storage area, Quinter looked at the light stanchion. It was still two hundred feet to the west. "Whew!" he whistled softly to himself, "that's one tough shot."

Kneeling on both knees and holding the Mauser with two hands, he sighted along the barrel and was beginning to tighten his finger on the trigger when he caught the flash of the Seát's lights out of the corner of his right eye.

Quickly, he moved back along the front of the building to the entranceway and flattened himself into the doorway. The lights of the approaching vehicle played along the side of the road as it came up the hill and around the curve, passing along the building in which he was hiding, and then disappearing into the brighter intensity of the storage area.

Quinter returned to the corner and once again placed the light in his sights. The Mauser recoiled slightly as the gun fired, but the light remained burning. On the second shot the glass shattered and the light sputtered out.

Patrolman Dunsos was opening the guardhouse door when he heard the distant pop of breaking glass and saw the area become darker. Lobos, the German Sheppard, stiffened and cocked his head toward the east in the direction of the noise. Dunsos pushed the door open. The Sergeant was asleep in his chair with his feet up on his desk and his chin on his chest, holding his half-full coffee mug in his lap.

"Sir." Dunsos began, "one of the lights just blew out. I think we should check it."

"Of course, officer," said Dellanzo who, though jolted from his rest did not spill a drop of his coffee. "Probably nothing, but we'll play safe. If there's a problem, Lobos will know." The two men left the guardhouse and started toward the north-eastern corner of the yard.

Quinter was watching the two police officers come from behind the guard station when he saw the animal. *Damn*, he thought. *I hadn't counted on a dog.* He moistened his right forefinger in his mouth, and held it up, noting with relief that the breeze was blowing from the west, toward him. *At least he won't smell me from this direction.*

The officers reached the base of the light standard, and stood looking up at the shattered lens 30 feet above.

"Strange," muttered Dellanzo. "I have not seen that happen before. Must have been a bad bulb."

"Probably so," mused Dunsos, as he played his flashlight along the seven foot chain link fence which had been bathed in darkness. "The fence looks O.K."

Dellanzo shone his light on the top of the fence, illuminating the five strands of barbed wire attached to metal brackets that led outward away from the fence at a rising angle. "Everything seems to be in order," he said, looking down at the Sheppard who was sitting placidly at the end of the leash Dunsos held in his left hand.

"Everything alright, boy?" The dog cocked his head in a futile effort to understand.

"Let's go back to the shack, and report this to maintenance." The officers swept the area one final time with their lights, and, satisfied, began walking back to the guardhouse.

Quinter watched them until they disappeared behind the guard station, noting with satisfaction that the thirty yards between the fence and the piled cargo at the tip of the diamond was now considerably less formidable. He waited in the shadows at the corner of the building for another five minutes to ensure that the guards had indeed cleared the area, and then moved cautiously to the fence, selecting a dark place.

Grasping the handles of the bolt cutter, he cut two sides of a two foot square, and pulled the section toward him. He lowered himself to a prone position, and wriggled through the hole, pausing only long enough to match the cut edges behind him, then took off in a crouched run toward the friendly cover of the nearest mountain. He glanced at his watch. 9:35. He'd have to work fast.

Using the piles of cargo to his advantage, Quinter leapfrogged from mountain to mountain until he arrived at the side of the warehouse. The dock gave him much better protection, and he could now see the outline of the upper superstructure of the huge ship.

The dimly-lit area was filled with stacked containers and crates, and equipment for lifting and moving. Quinter picked his way through the morass for a hundred and fifty yards, and, clearing the last obstacle, came face to face with the tanker amidships. He felt dwarfed by her size and scope. The ship was docked at the port side with her stern near the rear of the slip and her bow facing the open water beyond. A number of lights shone from cabin windows, and he saw a red glow coming from the bridge. He heard laughter off in the distance. It seemed to be coming from the deck near the base of the superstructure.

He scanned the length of the vessel. No gangplank was visible. A steel bridge twenty feet wide and forty feet long, still attached to the hook and cable of a large moveable crane, lay on the dock to his left, but other than the bow, spring, amidships, and stern lines, no contact existed between ship and land.

Quinter moved away from the voices and toward the bow and the sea, skirting the equipment and cargo. The voices were fading as he came nearer to the bow, and the moon broke through the clouds, casting light on the harbor for a few brief moments.

When he was near the spring line some fifty feet from the prow of the ship Quinter paused. His heart was racing, and adrenaline pulsed through his bloodstream. Looking out and up the line, he noticed a large circular metal plate in the shape of a cone attached to the line midway between the ship and the pier. *Probably some kind of vermin arrestor*, he thought, *I hope it's not effective against humans.*

He unzipped his small bag, removed a pair of black gloves, and quickly put them on. He adjusted the shoulder strap of the bag, drawing it close to his body, and grasped the heavy line. For ten feet, he pulled himself hand over hand across the water that rippled twenty feet below. When the cable began to make a steeper ascent, he locked his legs around it.

In a few minutes, he had reached the cone, and by a combined action of maneuvering himself around the barrier and pressing it upward against the cable with his body, continued his path toward the deck. The ship's handrail was still thirty feet above him. A few minutes later he was able to grab the deck railing and pull himself on board.

QUINTER

Quinter dropped into a crouch, and, his breath still coming in short heaves, and relaxed his arms to let the pain of fatigue drain from his shoulders, arms and hands.

From his position at the port railing of the foc'sle deck, Quinter had a clear view of the upper deck of the entire vessel. It was lined with a maze of intertwined pipes, valves, and pumping stations. As Quinter studied the tangle of equipment, he became aware of an open area about thirty-five feet in width stretching from the port railing to the middle of the ship around which all gear had been routed.

Quinter focused on the area and gradually realized the port side piping for no apparent mechanical reason crossed over to the starboard side, and then after a distance returned to its normal position on the port side.

Having recovered his wind—and his strength—Quinter climbed down a short ladder that led to the upper deck. A few minutes later, he made his way along catwalks and passages until he was standing at the edge of the open area which led directly to a large hatch cover some twenty-five feet wide and eighty feet long. A sturdy winch was located at the end of the hatch nearest to the starboard railing and the winch cable passed up and through a series of pulleys then down to the port side of the hatch. *That whole thing can be raised,* he thought.

Quinter walked to the forward side of the open space, and saw a small door. He hurried to it quickly and pressed down on the handle. "Damn!" he said softly when the handle wouldn't budge. Reaching inside the bag, he groped for his lock pick. Finding the tool, he inserted the pick in the lock. A full five minutes passed before he was able to disengage the tumblers, five minutes that seemed like an hour. At last, the final tumbler clicked and he depressed the handle opening the door.

156

Looking down, he saw a metal grating, onto which he stepped, leaving the door ajar. He listened carefully, his ears straining to catch the slightest sound, but all he could hear was the gentle lapping of the sea against ship structure. He smelled no unusual odors.

As his eyes adjusted to the darker environment, he looked down, and became aware of a dim light below. He pulled out a flashlight. As he played the beam around, he could see that the grating led to a series of metal steps which zigzagged back and forth. At each turn, the metal steps had a small metal landing. Quinter started cautiously down the steps. With each descending turn, the light below became brighter. After five turns, the steps ended at a door that was identical to the one Quinter had just opened. A low wattage bulb, surrounded by a metal wire cage, was above the opening. He pushed down on the handle, and, to his surprise, the door began to swing open.

Although it was pitch black except for the glow of the light over the door behind him, Quinter could tell he was in a large area. He pointed the beam of his flashlight up and saw a ramp suspended from the underside of the hatch by chains at one end and great hinges at the other. He directed the light to his right toward the stern of the ship, and there they were.

"Jesus," he whistled through clenched teeth, "Tanks. M-1 A-1 Tanks." The huge vehicles were parked in rows of five, five deep on either side of him. Their long gun barrels were covered with a protective material and the bodies had been painted in desert camouflage. "Those bastards!" he said softly to himself. "NATO my ass. Tanks! What a cover."

13

HELP!

J<small>ENNIFER HAD BEEN SITTING IN</small> the car for almost half an hour. Cleveland seemed a world away, not only in geography and time, but also in perspective. She had difficulty remembering that a little over a week ago her attention had been consumed by court dates, deposition times, client appointments and general administrative duties during the day. During the night, her life had been complicated by her unclear feelings for Quinter coupled with a general lack of direction or perhaps goals. Almost without thinking, she touched the side of her mouth where she'd been struck and felt the tiny bumps of knitted flesh under her skin. The emergency room doctor was right: there would be no scar, at least no physical scar.

Jennifer opened the door of the car and stepped outside into the night air. She peered up and down the road, noting with satisfaction there was neither traffic nor person in view. *The last thing I need is for someone to offer help,* she thought, as she looked closely at the lighted storage yard below.

The wind had calmed and the night air was fresh and cool. Preceded by the dog, a guard appeared from the guardhouse.

Officer Dunsos walked toward the tarped stack of cargo, which formed the head of the diamond, and then cut diagonally toward the warehouse. As he made the turn, he pointed the beam of his light along the darkened section of the fence passing a foot above the cut in the chain links. Lobos would have liked to continue, but allowed his course to be changed with little protest. A minute later, Dunsos disappeared behind the darkened corner of the warehouse.

Quinter crouched behind an air intake on the foc'sle deck near the spring line. He watched intently as Dunsos came into view following the same general path through the obstacles he had taken thirty minutes earlier. The dog was sniffing the ground and pulling on the leash.

"Easy, Lobos, easy," said Dunsos. "Do you have a scent?" The dog growled low in his throat and started pulling harder on the leash in the direction of the spring line and the bow of the ship. Dunsos gave ground and allowed the dog to have his head for the moment. Quinter laid flat on the deck watching the dog and man approach him. *Damn dog*, he thought again.

Lobos led his master to the pile around which the spring line was looped. He was still sniffing the ground and growling, the hair on the back of his neck bristling. Dunsos shined his light up the line, his eyes fixing on the ship above.

After thirty seconds he said, "Come on, Lobos. Probably a rat or some other small animal." Lobos resisted.

"Come Lobos!" Dunsos ordered, giving the dog a sharp yank on the leash, and the Sheppard reluctantly followed his master away from the ship and back to the guardhouse.

Quinter waited several minutes, put on the black gloves, and moved quickly to the spring line. In another several minutes he was on the pier retracing his steps to the warehouse, and soon he stood at the head of the diamond, thirty yards from safety. Giving one final glance in the direction of the guardhouse, Quinter made a break for the fence, pushing out the cut portion and wriggling through. Once again, he matched the cut portion to the fence, and picking up the bolt cutters from where he had left them in the shadows, raced to the corner of the building.

He ran toward the car, and seeing Jennifer leaning against the right front fender, yelled, "Jenny, get in. Let's get the hell out of here!"

Quinter slid in behind the wheel, threw his sack in the rear seat, and started the engine. He made a U-turn before switching on the lights. As the Seát moved down the curved incline, it passed Butler's green Volkswagen heading toward Seventeen West.

After a minute of silence, Quinter began, "Tanks, Jenny. New American M-1 tanks made by Nortex. *Fifty* of them loaded in a special cargo hold. These sons of bitches are selling the Iranians tanks in exchange for petro dollars or maybe crude oil. No question that the hold could easily be converted to carry crude. The Iraqis must have gotten wind of the plan somehow. Jenny, I wasn't kidding when I said we might be in the middle of a goddam Middle-Eastern war!"

"What should we do, Tom?" asked Jennifer, her voice trembling.

"I don't exactly know, honey, but I do know we need help. They're all going to be after us—especially when they find the hole in the fence, and they will soon," he answered in a rush of words. "We'll spend the night at the farm," Quinter continued after several seconds. "No one knows about the farm yet and we'll be safe."

GRAHAM BUTLER STOPPED the green Volkswagen at the security gate at the head of Seventeen West. He got out of the car, leaving the motor running and lights on as the two officers left the guard shack and came toward him. As they drew nearer, Sergeant Dellanzo unsnapped the leather strap securing his pistol in the holster. "This is a restricted area, sir," he said flatly.

"I understand," Butler replied, reaching for his wallet. Misinterpreting Butler's action, Dellanzo drew his pistol and leveled it at Butler's chest.

"Whoa," reacted Butler, quickly placing his hands in front of him, palms extended. "My identification. I'm Butler, Nortex security, Sergeant Dellanzo."

Dellanzo relaxed, lowering the pistol barrel. Slowly, Butler withdrew his wallet with his right hand and flipped it open, showing the officers the gold Nortex security badge.

An embarrassed Dellanzo holstered his weapon saying, "A thousand pardons, señor."

"No problem, Sergeant," answered Butler, looking out over the wide brightly lit storage area, his eyes coming to rest on the darkened far corner. "You could not have known. How many on duty tonight?"

"Myself and the patrolman. And, of course, the ship's crew, but no way to get aboard. They took the bridge down when they finished unloading this afternoon."

"The two of you," Butler repeated softly. "Anything unusual?

"Nothing. Oh, one of the lights blew out," answered Dellanzo.

"I noticed that. When did it happen," Butler inquired.

"About an hour ago. But we checked the scene, and no trouble was found. Time for the rounds. Would you like to come with me?" asked Dellanzo. "My turn this time." he said in Spanish to Dunsos, who had not understood a word of the conversation, but who comprehended the situation. "Give the señor your light and stay here to guard the gate." Dunsos handed his flashlight to Butler.

Butler and the Sergeant started out across the storage area and soon arrived at the cargo piled at the tip of the diamond. From this vantage point, Butler ran the beam of light along the base of the fence, passing over and then returning to the barely noticeable cut links. "You have had a visitor," he said in a forced tone as the two men approached the cut.

Butler knelt down on one knee, and with his left hand, pushed open the weakened section. He saw the grass had been disturbed, and pointed the area out to Dellanzo who was standing with his hands on his hips looking down, his brow furrowed.

"Can you get some more men?" said Butler, turning to the Sergeant. "This whole area should be searched."

"I'll call my superior," the Sergeant replied, and the two men quickly returned to the guardhouse.

IT WAS ELEVEN o'clock by the time Quinter pulled the Seát into the driveway of the farm. When he reached the end of the drive near the house, he did not stop, but took the tractor road heading toward the barn. The vehicle creaked and bumped as it labored over the uneven hard mud ruts. Arriving at the barn, Quinter continued around the side and parked so that the car would not be visible from the road. He turned off the engine and the parking lights, and then sat behind the wheel pondering the situation.

After a short while he said, "Jenny, I think our best bet is to call Jeff Downing."

"Can he help?"

163

"He has a lot of contacts, and we need to get some other people involved."

They walked to the house and pushed open the front door. Inside it was pitch black. Quinter fumbled for the switch on a lamp near the door, and finding it, flipped it on. The single low wattage bulb bathed the small living room and part of the dining room in dull yellow light.

Quinter pulled a dining room chair over to the small wooden table on which the telephone sat. He took Downing's number from his wallet and handed it to Jennifer.

"See if you can get Jeff on the line."

Jennifer handed telephone back. It rang eight times before the call was answered.

"Hello."

"Martha, this is Tom Quinter. Is Jeff there? I need help."

SERGEANT DELLANZO, PATROLMAN Dunsos, and five other officers of the Malaga Port Authority gathered at the end of the pier with Butler at the conclusion of their fruitless search. Butler assigned three men to the pier, two to the warehouse, and instructed Dellanzo and Dunsos to remain at the gate. Minutes earlier, he had spoken with the captain of the ship and had been informed there was no evidence of any unusual activity and everything was in order.

The men departed for their respective stations, and as Butler walked along the side of the vessel in the direction of the stern, a flood of outrage swelled inside him. He still could hardly believe the conversation he'd overheard at the villa. Butler decided that when the others arrived, he would make some excuse, return to La Herradura, search for any evidence that might exist, and report all he knew to the authorities. But which authorities? Certainly at least some elements of the government had to be involved in the plan.

He knew he was in a dangerous situation. Perhaps not *imminent* danger, not as long as the right people were around, but certainly potential danger. *The question*, he thought emphatically to himself, *is who are the good guys?* He began by thinking that his best move would be to tell the local police and then the local newspaper. Or maybe the other way around. There was no sense in getting tied up with police bureaucracy before the word got out. He wouldn't use a small town. His information would have more impact and was less likely to get buried in a larger city. Malaga probably.

He made up his mind to do it in the morning, after investigating the villa tonight. "Damn!" he whispered through his teeth. "I need some hard evidence. Where the hell is Quinter?"

Butler reached the rudder of the *Crescent* just as a black Mercedes entered the driveway, followed by the Citroën. The two cars parked next to the guard house. Bordman got out of the Mercedes as the two Iranians and Abdullah, left the Citroën. After speaking with the officers at the gate, the men began walking toward the ship. Butler heard the sound of an electric motor above and behind him, followed by the creak of metal on metal, as the gangplank began to telescope down from the ship toward the pier.

"Hello, Graham," said Bordman, his words slightly slurred.

"Good evening, Mr. Bordman," replied Butler.

"Understand you may have had some activity," continued Bordman.

"Possible, Sir. Hard to tell. But someone cut the fence. Maybe not tonight."

"Well, Graham, seems as if you have everything under control. Why don't you take a little time before we meet you back in La Herradura? Go out for a coffee. See the city. We'll be about an hour, and will meet you back at the villa. No point in your hanging around here anymore."

"Certainly, Sir," answered Butler noting that he was again being excluded but thinking how, for once, Bordman's orders coincided perfectly with his plans. He started walking toward the guardhouse and the green Volkswagen.

The end of the gangplank touched the wooden pier and slid three feet to rest. "Come gentlemen," said Bordman to the group, "shall we have a look?"

As the group began up the metal walkway toward the deck of the ship, Mr. Maziar grasped Abdullah's sleeve and whispered in Farsi, "Follow him. I want to know where he goes and what he does. I would not miss him if he were never to be seen again."

"I understand, my master," hissed Abdullah.

USING THE ODDLY shaped triangular key Butler unlocked the heavy wooden door. At the top of the pathway leading down to the darkened villa, he stopped to turn on the walkway lights, which illuminated the descending walk through the gardens. He closed and bolted the door behind him, and with a deliberate speed, proceeded down the walk. The night was dark and calm although occasionally a brief flicker of moonlight appeared through the clouds.

He found the kitchen door unlocked, pushed it open and turned on the light. At the same deliberate pace, he walked down the hallway past the artwork, toward the back hall and Bordman's room. When he reached the room, he began a methodical search that shortly uncovered Bordman's briefcase in the bottom bureau drawer. He sat down on the bed with it and pulled out a sheaf of papers.

"Shipping documents," he mused, "a set for the *Crescent* and one for the Eastern *Star*. Munitions of some sort."

This was not unexpected, he thought as he flipped through the first few pages. His study was interrupted by sudden buzzing of the telephone. His mind raced. Should he answer it? Bordman would not be happy that he had returned to the villa so soon. Before he had thought through all the possibilities, he found himself moving rapidly toward the telephone on the living room table.

"Hello," he answered firmly.

"Graham, this is Quinter."

Butler felt a flood of relief. "Tom," he blurted, "you're expendable. They're going to kill you and Jennifer."

"Those bastards and that bastard Bordman. I was afraid they'd reached that point. Listen Graham, the *Crescent* is loaded with tanks—fifty goddamn M-1 tanks. I've seen them. I think they're headed to Iran—perhaps in exchange for oil. That's what this Energia division is all about. Everything fits. We've got to stop them."

"Jesus," exclaimed Butler. "I thought it might you who cut the fence. Where are you, Tom?"

"Jenny and I are at a farm, located out MA 405 toward Campanillas. About seven kilometers from the limits of Malaga. It's across the road from a country church. Telephone number is 45-384. I'll call and tell Bordman in the morning before we leave. At least we'll know where they'll take the goods they've off-loaded. I've asked a friend, Jeff Downing, for help. He's working on an answer."

"Tom, I just found some shipping documents for the tankers. Haven't had a chance to go through them in any detail. I plan to go to the papers and local police in Malaga tomorrow, if I can't come up with a better way. This may be enough evidence to persuade them to board the ship."

"Good," replied Quinter acceding to Butler's security instincts. "I'll have heard back from Downing by then. Jennifer and I are using a hotel in Almuñécar, La Regencia, as a contact point in case we get separated, using our mothers' maiden names. Hers is Rose, mine Andros."

"Mine's Lujack. Betty Ann Lujack. Those creeps will be getting back here, and I'd better be going. I'll spend the night at La Regencia, and leave a message for you tomorrow. Take care, Tom, They're a nasty lot."

"You take care too, Graham."

Butler hung up the phone and returned to Bordman's bedroom, stopping first at his own room to grab a suitcase. He took a small camera from the suitcase and laid the documents out on the floor, photographing each one in sequence. He then replaced the papers in the briefcase and returned it to the drawer. Butler took one last gaze around the room, and, satisfied everything was in order, turned off the light and closed the door.

He walked up the path toward the wooden door, turning off the path light at the top of the steps, a ray of moonlight flashing over the garden as he did so. Unbolting the door, he stepped outside onto the street, and then turned around to lock the door.

The blow crashed into Butler's back directly between his shoulder blades, driving him to his hands and knees on the asphalt. He felt the light cord wrap around his neck and he made an involuntary gasping wheeze as it shut off his air and the blood flow to his head. As he made a desperate futile attempt to grasp the biting cord with his left hand, he struggled to get to his feet.

His senses reeling, he reached behind him with his right hand and felt the hard flat stomach muscles of his assailant. Slowly and almost gently, he slid his hand down inside the

168

loose pantaloons, across the man's penis, grabbing hold of his testicles as a bright red light began flashing in front of his eyes. He imbedded his fingernails in the soft loose flesh and the light began to dim and blink. His assailant screamed with pain and tried to tighten the cord around Butler's neck.

With adrenaline flooding through his blood vessels, Butler ripped and tore at the flesh repeatedly, now feeling a warm sticky fluid ooze between his fingers each time he applied all of his strength. Suddenly the remaining skin gave way and his arm and hand broke free of the pantaloons.

The cord became slack as Abdullah grasped his groin, and shrieking howls of pain and terror, jumped up and down with both feet leaving the ground as he turned in circles.

Butler fell to the ground. Regaining a degree of consciousness, he saw Abdullah, now howling like a mad dog, prone on the pavement rolling first in one direction and then the other, his hands seemingly glued to his bloody crotch. Butler struggled to his feet. His right fist, still clenched, was drenched with blood. He opened it slowly and saw the mass of bloody skin and tissue. A wave of nausea and disgust swept over him, and he threw the mass at Abdullah as he vomited.

"You fucker!" Butler gurgled through the vomit. A berserk Abdullah struggled to his feet, screaming nonsensically and, weaving from side to side, shuffled down the road in a stooped-over gait, pressing the bright red wet cloth between his legs to his body with both hands. Butler staggered to the green Volkswagen, fumbled open the door, and collapsed into the driver's seat. Moments later, he started the engine, and began driving up the hill toward Almuñécar.

QUINTER WAS JOLTED from a fitful sleep by the jangle of the telephone. He sat up on the bed, collected himself, and then rose and walked over to the ringing phone. "Yes," he said without a trace of emotion.

"Tom, this is Jeff. They're listening to us. Go to Grenada and meet Richard Deacon at the Alhambra in the Courtyard of the Lions at noon tomorrow. I've told him Butler is on our side. Deacon's CIA. He'll be wearing a red bandanna, and will listen to your story."

"Listen to my story, shit!" exploded Quinter. "We've got to get the right people on that ship!"

"We tried, Tom, but the *Crescent* sailed at one o'clock this morning, your time. The navy will get on it at daylight, and Suez has been notified."

Quinter looked at his watch. It was three o'clock in the morning.

"Jesus," he groaned. "All right, Deacon at the Alhambra tomorrow at noon. We're using La Regencia hotel in Almuñécar as a contact point. Again, my alias is Andros, Jennifer's is Rose. By the way, thanks Jeff, I don't mean to sound ungrateful."

"I understand, Tom. Keep in touch. Bye."

Quinter replaced the telephone, returned to the bed and collapsed once more into fitful sleep.

14

FUGITIVES

AFTER A REFRESHING COOL SHOWER, Quinter toweled himself dry, and, wrapping the towel tightly around his waist, walked into the living room. Jennifer was sitting on the sofa, her chin in her hands.

"Your turn, honey," he said.

Without saying a word, Jennifer got up from the sofa and the two stood facing one another.

"Tom," she said, as he put his arms around her and held her, "we'll be fine."

"Sure," he replied as he smoothed her warm, wavy hair on the back of her head. "I think the tables are beginning to turn in our direction. This Deacon fellow has access, and can get us to the right people."

Jennifer raised her head from his shoulder, and walked toward the shower as Quinter pulled on a pair of rumpled khakis.

"I'm going to phone Bordman now, Jenny, so we should be out of here in fifteen minutes," he called out to her.

Quinter dialed the number for Quinta de la Torre. His watch told him it was 8:00 o'clock.

The telephone rang several times before Quinter heard a voice say, "Hello."

"This is Quinter."

"Good morning Tom. This is Ralph Jones. How are you?"

"Fine, Ralph, and you?" Quinter said.

"Good. Would you like to talk to Dave?"

"Please." A few moments of silence passed.

"Hello, Tom. How are you, and what's up?" Bordman began smoothly.

"Things have been a little hectic, but Jenny and I have enjoyed our stay in Malaga. Beautiful city," Quinter replied.

"Good. I trust you have found a farm. The plan calls for us to store some equipment as soon as possible. My people in Madrid tell me the damn pacifists are getting all kinds of media attention, and they've even got a member of parliament for a spokesman. We've got to move. No telling when they'll discover we've landed the goods in Malaga. In fact, the trucks are being loaded at the port as we speak. Where are you calling from?"

"Well," Quinter answered, cautiously, "as a matter of fact, I'm speaking to you from the farm. Good place. Sits on a hill. Beautiful view of the coast and Malaga off to the east. A little run-down, perhaps, but comfortable. Jenny and I spent last night here."

"Excellent. Where is it located?"

"Just east of a little town called Campanillas on MA 405. On the west side of the road, across from a country church. Has a white barn behind the stucco farmhouse. Set back off the road about a quarter of a mile. The phone number is 45-384. You can't miss it. It's the only one around. Seven kilometers west of Malaga."

"Good work, Tom. I'm going to send the trucks right away. I guess you've about completed your mission. Where will you and Jenny be staying?"

"Don't know just yet, Dave. We'll probably ride around a bit today, and then find a place to stay tonight. We'll give you a call when we get settled."

"Fine, Tom," said Bordman, masking his disappointment at failing to determine Quinter's destination. "You and Jenny must join us for dinner tonight. There's a good beach restaurant in La Herradura, I think it's called Chiringuito Juaquán. Would love to give you two a bit of a send-off."

"Sounds like it will be an interesting party. We'll look forward to it."

"Haven't seen Butler for a while. Have you?

"Nope."

"By the way, how's the little Seát operating? Some of these Spanish products, you know . . .," Bordman said casually, failing to complete the sentence.

"Fine, Dave. How did you know the car?" asked Quinter, displaying only polite curiosity.

"Let's see, oh, José Luís told me. I rented a couple of cars from him and gave the Quinta de la Torre address. He made the connection. Tom, give me a call as soon as you know your plans. Until tonight, then."

"Bye Dave." and Quinter hung up.

"Come on, Jenny. We have ten minutes to clear out!"

Exactly ten minutes later, Quinter and Jennifer were driving northeast heading toward Campanillas. Looking for a place to eat, they spotted a small cafe nestled in the side of one of the foothills of the Burgo Mountains. Quinter pulled into the small dirt parking lot and parked next to two other vehicles. The café was clean and neat. White tablecloths with blue borders covered each of the six round tables, and the three small square tables along the front windows of the café, covered with white tablecloths with dark maroon borders, were set for two. Each overlooked the sandy-brown foothills that descended in undulating tiers to the Malaga coast. The hills were dotted with darker green trees and the sun was well up in the clear blue cloudless morning sky.

The pleasant young waitress seated Quinter and Jennifer at the center window table, and then returned with two steaming mugs of coffee.

"Would you like to order?" she asked.

"I'm famished," said Quinter. "For me, scrambled eggs, ham, potatoes, toast—the works."

Jennifer gave the order to the waitress, and as an afterthought, asked her for one of the newspapers stacked on the counter near the cash drawer. When the waitress left, Jennifer looked at Quinter.

"What's the game plan?"

"I'm not a hundred percent sure," Quinter answered. "Of course, we'll meet Deacon at noon, and perhaps he'll have some ideas. But if we get no help, I think the key concept is to follow Butler's lead. He's going to the media and the local police. I could contact some of my old friends at Davis-James, they might have some thoughts. The problem is that it's my word and whatever documents Butler obtains against the whole damn Nortex organization, certain elements of the Spanish government, and of course the Iranians."

The waitress returned with the newspaper and the croissant Jennifer had ordered. Jennifer broke off a piece of the pastry and opened the paper. Quinter took a sip of the strong black coffee. Suddenly, the headline of an article in the lower left-hand corner of the front page screamed at her: "American Couple Sought for Questioning in Brutal Murders."

"Tom, Tom," she said, her voice low and filled with urgency, "the police are looking for us!" She quickly scanned the remainder of the article. "It's all here."

"Easy, honey," Quinter said, ignoring the growing lump in his chest. "What does it say?"

"Let's see. A man was beaten to death in Madrid. And the bodies of two foreign nationals washed up on the beach just east of Almuñécar. An undisclosed American company provided information that one of their employees, an American national, and a female traveling companion were in the vicinity of the killings—and the employee had a history of mental instability. Jesus! Apparently another employee, one of the company's security people, may also be involved."

"Sweet folks," Quinter said clenching his teeth. "Bordman always was a believer in narrowing his opponent's options. We sure can't take our case to the cops. Deacon's our best—and maybe only—shot. Enjoy your breakfast. It may be our last one on the outside. Good thing the Spanish don't believe in capital punishment for women," he said, making a feeble attempt at humor. Jennifer scowled.

"We'll finish up here, casually, and head for Granada. The timing ought to be just about right."

The waitress arrived with Quinter's food, and he ate with relish.

It was nine o'clock by the time Quinter headed the Seát southeast on MA-401 back toward Malaga. Even though traffic was extremely light, he and Jennifer decided to take the back roads to Granada. The time and distance might be a little longer, but the chance of discovery was far less.

Passing the farmhouse where they'd spent the night, they noted, with a mixture of satisfaction and relief, that there was no sign of any activity.

As the car began a long steep descent, Quinter noticed a column of army trucks covered with canvas grinding up the hill in the other direction. Great plumes of black smoke belched from the vertical exhausts attached on the rear of the cabs as the engines labored up the grade. Preceding the column were two cars with the markings of the Spanish National Police.

"I'll bet those are our boys," said Quinter, as he began to pass the convoy, slowing down for a better look. "How many do you count, Jenny?"

"Eleven," she replied after a minute, "and two more police type cars at the end."

Sᴇʀɢᴇᴀɴᴛ Dᴇʟʟᴀɴᴢᴏ ʜᴀᴅɴ'ᴛ slept well, not getting to bed until almost 1:30 in the morning. He was irritated at having received orders to be at work by 7:30 to escort some convoy into the hills, and to be the trailing vehicle at that. He watched the procession of heavy trucks move slowly up the incline and kept as much distance as he dared in order to avoid the dense black smoke.

Patrolman Dunsos was asleep in the passenger seat, and the only sound the Sergeant was able to hear, other than the whine of the diesel engines and the incessant crackle of static on the police radio, was Dunsos' snoring. The entire situation offended his notion of what a Sergeant's position should entail.

Perhaps because the vehicle was traveling too slowly for a down grade, or perhaps because he had a dim recollection from his early morning briefing of some reference by his commanding officer to be on the alert for a green Seát, his attention was drawn to an approaching car. Instinctively, as the car passed, he noted the color, made a mental note of the license plate, and grabbed the microphone to report the vehicle to the dispatcher.

176

In less than thirty seconds his radio blared, "Car number 47. Desist from your present assignment immediately and follow the Seát. Repeat, follow the Seát immediately. Do not intercept. Repeat, do not intercept, but follow the Seát and report."

"Understood," replied Dellanzo, his juices beginning to flow, "Follow the Seát and report only. No interception."

"That's affirmative," the dispatcher answered. "Keep me closely posted."

"Yes, Sir, and out."

Dellanzo put the microphone back on the hook while bringing the car to an abrupt stop on the pavement, shocking patrolman Dunsos into the world of the wide awake. He looked in the rear view mirror. Noting there was no traffic behind him, he made a boot-leg turn on the road, and sped after the Seát which had disappeared around the curve at the bottom of the hill.

"What's going on?" asked Dunsos, his voice thick with sleep.

A grin spreading across his face, the Sergeant answered, "We just got a better assignment."

QUINTER AND JENNIFER had been following MA-340 for about three-quarters of an hour as the highway looped and twisted through the Almijara Mountains.

As the morning warmed, they opened all the car's windows, and the mountain air felt fresh and delightfully cool. Puffy white clouds were just beginning to develop over the easterly edge of the tallest peaks. The vehicle climbed from crest to valley in its gradual course upward, passing through the little mountain villages of Colmenar and Periana, as they neared Alhama de Granada.

The town, like so many others, was constructed around the public square. On its perimeter were various mercantile establishments. The square was dominated by a substantial church. Along both sides of the narrow street were rows of white alabaster houses with red tile roofs, each sharing a wall with its neighbor. Dogs and children romped and played in the doorways and alleys, and the women and old men stood or sat in their respective groups conversing.

Quinter continued driving northeast at a leisurely pace, down toward the small city of Armilla. He was occasionally, and dimly, aware of a vehicle in the distance behind him, but nothing about the situation caused him any alarm. He looked over toward Jennifer who had reclined the seat mid-way and was either resting with her eyes closed or sleeping.

You are such a beautiful woman, he thought, as he followed the curve of her breasts. *And a friend. You, my love, are a real "pal"*, he mused to himself. *I guess I just needed some time to figure out what's important. Careful, Quinter,* he chided himself, *let's not go overboard. But what the heck, you love this lady, and you might as well just face the fact.* He smiled as he connected with his growing feeling of fulfillment.

It was 11:30 as Quinter and Jennifer entered Granada. Jennifer had to ask for directions three different times before they were able to locate the Cuesta de Gomárez, which led up to the Alhambra. The Cuesta de Gomárez ended at the Gate of the Pomegranates entrance, where Quinter parked the car.

Hand in hand, they walked through the gate and passed a marble cross. The urban setting immediately dissolved into woodland full of greenery and shadows. The singing of birds and the murmuring trickle of slowly moving water replaced the noise of the city. They continued to walk a short distance up the road until they came to the fountain of Charles V, beyond which they could see the massive block-like structure through which had been built the Gate of Justice.

As they walked through the gate into the interior of the Alhambra, Quinter turned and said, "Jenny, this is the Gate of Justice. Jesus, I hope this Deacon fellow is for real."

"So do I," she replied, "so do I."

15

THE ALHAMBRA

QUINTER AND JENNIFER WALKED THROUGH the Gate of Justice, around the Palace of Carlos V, entering the Court of the Myrtles. The courtyard, centered by a narrow 150 foot long rectangular reflecting pool bordered by a white marble walkway, was open to the sky. At either end, seven elongated semicircular arches were supported by single columns. The center of the middle arch, the largest, lined up with the middle of the pool. The plaster facades of the arches were decorated in diamond and other more intricate patterns. Behind the columns of the arches was a corridor.

On the far side, a wall separated the courtyard from adjoining quarters. The top of the wall repeated, in another form, the carvings on the face of the arches, and the bottom, which was inlaid with many small differently colored tiles, again featured the diamond motif. A broad white band of alabaster separated the formed brown plaster at the top of the wall from the inlaid tile at the bottom. A red tile roof covered the corridors on all four sides, and each end of the pool was crowned with a square military tower complete with battlements.

Occasionally, small groups of people wandered through the arches and corridors pointing out particular patterns and speaking in quiet voices.

"This is amazing," said Quinter as he turned and looked back through a succession of arches in the direction from which they had just come.

"It's so beautiful and not easy to understand," said Jennifer. "Those are myrtle hedges which line the pool on either side. The arches and spandrels are purely decorative, but the columns support pilasters that in turn support the lintels. Everything is horizontal and vertical in the classic Greek tradition."

"Is that so? Where did you learn that?"

"I had a terrific architecture course in school. Anything else you would like to know?" she said, teasing him nonchalantly.

The couple stood for a few minutes looking north across the length of the pool at the squat rectangular tower framed in the elongated arch nearest them, and then out through a series of arches to the hills beyond. Then they followed the rear corridor into the Court of the Lions, a courtyard that was also rectangular in shape and open to the sky. A series of symmetrical single and double columns with complex designs carved and shaped on the plaster faces surrounded the area. Two perpendicular marble walkways divided the courtyard into quarters and white stone gravel filled each quarter.

At the point in the center where the walks intersected, a large circular fountain with a single plume of water was supported by twelve grotesque lions, their teeth bared, and their tails uniformly wrapped around their left hind quarters. As if to make a mockery of the trappings of power, a single small jet of water exited playfully from the open mouths of each of the beasts and splashed into a circular channel below.

Quinter and Jennifer walked along the south corridor until they came to the midpoint. They stopped, looked out across the fountain to the far side of the court and saw a man wearing blue jeans and a long-sleeved white cotton shirt with the cuffs turned up leaning against one of the double sets of columns. Around his neck was a red bandanna.

Quinter motioned to Jennifer to remain in the corridor and started out the marble walk toward the fountain. As he did so, the man also began walking toward the center of the court. When they reached their respective sides of the fountain, they stopped, as if by pre-arrangement.

"Quinter?" the man asked.

"Richard Deacon?"

"Yes," he replied.

Richard Deacon was middle-aged, with a round face topped with thin blond hair receding at the hairline. Almost six feet tall, he was somewhat overweight, yet he had a solid build and was obviously in good condition. His physical presence gave the impression of a direct and secure person.

"Downing tells me you are to be considered a friend," Quinter began, and then beckoned to Jennifer over his shoulder.

"My understanding is the same," Deacon answered smiling slightly. "I've been told you have some shipping information for me."

"Yes. The Nortex *Crescent* off-loaded a shipment of arms, but I've seen the rest of the cargo. She carries fifty M-1 A-1 tanks for *someone*. I suspect you folks will not be pleased, since it seems the Iranians are involved."

"Someone told us it might be a contraband swap for oil. Maybe you did, Mr. Quinter."

"That *is* my thought. Butler may have some documentation, but I haven't seen it. I'm told the *Crescent* got away early this morning."

"True," said Deacon. "That's a problem we're trying to fix. I understand from Mr. Butler that another Nortex ship is due in Malaga tomorrow."

"I think so. Richard, I hope you people intend to take some action."

"We're quite interested, Mr. Quinter, excuse me, Tom. It seems the Nortex folks may have manufactured a few more of these tanks than called for by the production quotas. We're still checking. Haven't been on this very long, you understand."

Quinter nodded.

"In the meantime, Tom, we think you, and Miss Millieux- is that correct? . . ."

Jennifer nodded.

". . .Miss Millieux should go to Madrid and check in with the American embassy there. They'll be expecting you, and I understand there are arrangements to fly you back to the States right away. First to Washington for a day or so, and then to Cleveland. We also believe there are some people who would like to get their hands on you. They think you are a liability. However, we don't believe they are yet aware of our interest."

A young couple and two children approached the fountain. Using his hands, the five year old began trying to redirect the spray of water flowing from the small jet coming from one of the enraged lions. Quinter, Deacon, and Jennifer edged around to the other side of the fountain.

"It feels damned unresolved to me," said Quinter. "These bastards sucker me into this deal, just about get us killed, and now you tell me I should pick up my marbles and go home."

184

"I understand your feelings, Mr. Quinter," said Deacon almost kindly, "but, trust me, it's best to let us handle the matter from here on out, as there is no question things will get nasty. There's a lot hanging in the balance for some very powerful people."

"I know," Quinter replied. "Frankly, the whole affair pisses me off, but you're right, so Jenny and I will play tourist for another hour or so, and then we'll be off to Madrid."

"It's for the best. Here's where you can reach me." Deacon handed Quinter a card and then thrust his right hand forward. "I run a messenger service, you know. The lady who answers the phone is one of ours." The two men shook hands.

"So long, Mr. Quinter. Pleasure to have met you, Miss Millieux."

With that, Deacon left the Court of the Lions. Quinter gave Deacon's card to Jennifer, and she quickly copied the number before returning it.

"You never know, it might be a good idea to keep this handy" he said.

"I agree," she answered.

Sᴇʀɢᴇᴀɴᴛ Dᴇʟʟᴀɴᴢᴏ ᴀɴᴅ patrolman Dunsos had been waiting outside the Gate of the Pomegranates for about thirty minutes. After the Sergeant had reported the location of the green Seát to the dispatcher, he'd been instructed to remain outside the Alhambra and report any further events.

This is interesting business, he thought, but still wondering why he had not been asked to make the arrest if the occupants of the vehicle were in fact wanted persons. *Certainly, I am qualified, and an arrest would certainly look good on my record for promotion next year.*

The policeman's thoughts were interrupted by the arrival of a black BMW sedan that pulled up behind him. Four men got out. The driver took out his wallet, and flipping it open displayed the government issued security badge.

"Sergeant, I'm Taminos of the National Security Police."

"Yes sir," responded Dellanzo as he opened the door of his car, realizing something important was happening. "I'm Sergeant Dellanzo of the Malaga Port Authority. This is officer Dunsos." The men shook hands.

"Are the suspects still in the Alhambra?" asked Taminos.

"Yes sir, and that's their car," he pointed to the Seát.

"Thanks Sergeant. Good work. We have the matter under control now. You may return to your base in Malaga, Sergeant."

"Thank you, sir," said Dellanzo unable to mask his disappointment.

"You're welcome, Sergeant. I'll make a good report for your file. This will not go unnoticed."

"Oh, thank you, sir," said Dellanzo showing renewed enthusiasm. "And Officer Dunsos as well?"

"And Officer Dunsos," said Taminos.

Dellanzo and Dunsos returned to their car to begin the trip back to Malaga.

QUINTER AND JENNIFER strolled along the walkways on the top of the wall that joined the towers. From time to time, they paused to enjoy the idyllic view of the Sierra Nevada Mountains, in clear view and majestic in their grandeur.

Jennifer was having a hard time accepting that soon they would be on a plane headed home. For his part Quinter also felt anxious. He understood, and accepted, that Deacon was right in asking them to go as that would take them out of harm's way. Quinter also realized that in fact there was little he or Jennifer could do. But he had been used, and was angry he would not get to play a personal part in the conclusion of the affair. *My friend, Bordman,* he thought. *Some friend. What a snake.*

"Well, Jenny, shall we walk back through the gardens and then leave for Madrid?"

"I guess so, Tom," she answered wistfully. And then added quietly, "I love you."

"I love you too," he replied, his voice thick with emotion. The couple embraced and held each other tightly.

After a while, they began walking back toward the Gate of Justice. As they neared the gate, Quinter excused himself to use the restroom. "I'll be just a minute," he said.

Jennifer said, smiling, "Let me have the keys and I'll meet you at the car."

Jennifer walked through the Gate of Justice, past the fountain, and through the wooded area down toward the Gate of the Pomegranates.

Still smiling, she realized that this was the first time in several days that she had been separated from Quinter. She joyfully hummed to herself, even skipped a few steps, and walked ostentatiously swinging her hips as she put the Gate behind her. Several cars were parked in the gate parking lot, but no people were in sight. She unlocked the door, sat in the driver's seat, and placed the key in the ignition. Then she turned on the radio.

Sitting in the BMW sedan with his three fellow officers, Security officer Taminos saw Jennifer as she came through the gate. Clearly, she was heading toward the Seát.

"Damn, where's the señor?" he asked out loud.

"Look, she's starting the engine. She's going to leave," said one of his companions.

Taminos thought for a few seconds. "We'll take her now and the man later," he ordered, hoping he was making the right decision. "You two come with me!" he told the two men in the rear seat. "Francisco, you wait with the car."

The trio of plain-clothes policemen approached the driver's side of the Seát. Taminos pulled his wallet from the pocket of his jacket and flashed the National Security badge.

"Señorita, National Security Police. You will come with us now," he ordered in broken but understandable English.

"What is the meaning of this?" Jennifer demanded.

"I said come with us now," repeated Taminos opening the door and taking hold of Jennifer's left arm. When she resisted, Taminos pulled her from the vehicle.

She tried to scream, but at the first sound, one of the men covered her mouth with his hand, and, working together, the three men picked her up, and carried her, kicking and protesting, to the BMW. With one man on either side of her, they threw her in the car.

"She's a hellcat," groaned Taminos rubbing his right shin where Jennifer had kicked him. "Tape and cuff her."

Francisco ripped a piece of adhesive tape from the roll and roughly taped it over Jennifer's mouth. One of the men held her hands behind her back while the other snapped on a set of handcuffs. After Jennifer had been subdued, Taminos muttered to himself, "Now, señor, your turn."

Five minutes passed then ten, and soon fifteen. Still, there was no sign of the señor. Taminos turned around and addressed Jennifer now sitting quietly in the middle of the rear seat. "He is coming back, shortly, señorita?"

Jennifer shook her head.

"You will tell us what we want to know, señorita. It will be easier if you tell us here. It will be much more difficult if we must go to the hotel and get the Doctor. You will tell us now, señorita?"

Jennifer nodded her head in seeming agreement.

"Remove the tape Francisco, but be careful," said Taminos.

The tape was removed and Jennifer took a deep breath. "He's gone to meet a friend at Generalife. They are leaving together, and I'm to meet them later," she lied.

"Where are you to meet," asked Taminos suspiciously.

"At the restaurant of the hotel we passed on the way to the Alhambra. I do not know the city well," she said evenly.

"Why are you telling me this?" he continued, his suspicion unassuaged.

"Because I think you would hurt me if I didn't. I don't think you will hurt him. At least, not now," she replied.

"An intelligent woman," he said. "We'll wait a little longer, however."

QUINTER HAD WATCHED Jennifer pass through the Gate of the Pomegranates, and he felt joy in his heart as he saw her walk across the parking area. But his joy turned to fear and then rage when the three men assaulted her and carried her off. If he had brought his weapon, he might have tried to prevent it, and perhaps hurt them all, but he did see the one man offer his identification—and there was no assurance that Jennifer would not be injured in any attack.

He moved to just outside the most southerly opening through the gate, and putting the wall between him and his opponents view of his advance, worked his way to the wall.

Within a few moments, he was close enough to the BMW so that he could read the license plate. Reading 4F-196, he knew it was a federally-issued plate and had to force down his fear and rage even further. If he were to be effective, he would have to think and act coolly.

He crouched behind the wall and waited. The next move would be up to his hunters.

AFTER HALF AN hour had passed, and there was still no sign of the señor, Taminos weighed the possibilities. Perhaps the señorita was telling the truth and the señor would not return, a thought which now seemed distinctly possible. Perhaps, on the other hand, she was merely protecting him, and after some appropriate interval, he would conclude the visit with his friend and return. He decided to cover both scenarios.

"Francisco, you and the others take the lady back in the BMW to the Alhambra Palace Hotel. I will wait here to see whether the señor returns or not."

"Very good, Sir. Do you think that you can handle him if he comes back?" asked Francisco.

"He will have no reason to suspect anything is amiss until too late," answered Taminos. "Take her to the room, but don't harm her. I will be with you within the hour. The keys to the Seát are still in the ignition?"

"Yes Sir. Just as we left them."

"Good Francisco. When you have secured the lady, drive back and pick me up. By that time I should have the señor under control. We'll worry about his car later. Move quickly now."

As TAMINOS OPENED the door and got out of the BMW, Quinter was watching him from his vantage point. He saw one of the officers slide over to the driver's seat, and start the engine. He made a U-turn, and quickly left the area. The apparently more senior officer walked fifty feet over to the other side of the parking area opposite the parked Seát, sat down on the low curb, and took a pocket knife from his side pocket. He picked up a small branch, and opening the knife, began to whittle.

Quinter surveyed the scene, concluding the cover was perfect for surprising the officer. He glanced back up the walkway and saw two middle-aged women approaching. Calculating that he could use their arrival as a distraction, he crossed two openings in the Gate and ducked through the third, concealing himself behind the thick shrubbery. From there, he worked his way gradually down the parking area, using the shrubs to shield himself from view, until he had reached a position behind the whittling man.

The officer was looking to his left toward the gate in the direction of the voices as the women walked through the gate, got in their car, and drove off. Taminos continued to whittle; about fifteen feet directly behind him, Quinter waited. A car drove into the far end of the lot, parked in front of the Seát and cut its engine. A couple emerged and kissed in a passionate embrace. The officer looked at the couple and smiled.

This was Quinter's moment.

"Do you have a match, señor?" he asked.

Taminos, startled by the sound of a voice so near him, turned to his right as a perfectly timed blow from Quinter's knee caught him full on the right cheek and knocked him senseless to the ground. Quinter bent over the fallen man, to open his jacket, and remove his wallet.

"Ignacio Taminos, Spanish National Security Police, number 3541," Quinter said to himself. "Well, Mr. National Security Policeman, that one's for my lady." Taminos moaned. Quinter walked to the Seát, and finding the keys in the ignition, started the car. Without hesitation, he drove out of the parking area, down the road past the Alhambra Palace Hotel and toward the city below.

At the bottom of the hill, he made several turns in order to get off the main traveled route, and stopped at the first public telephone. He dialed the number on the card Deacon gave him, and listened intently to the ringing signal.

"Hello, Deacon's Messenger Service," the female voice answered in Spanish.

"Do you speak English? Is Deacon in?"

"Yes I do, and no Sir. But I expect him soon. Are you one of his clients?"

"You're damn right I'm one of his clients. Tell him four thugs from the Spanish National Security Police have taken Jennifer—he'll remember her—God knows where. Ignacio Taminos, badge number 3541. Black BMW, plate number 4F-196. Tell him to do something right away. And tell him I have a score to settle on the Costa del Sol. He can reach me at La Regencia Hotel in Almuñécar under the name of Andros. You get all that?"

"Yes Sir," the voice replied calmly.

"Good. Now say everything back to me." Quinter listened, and, satisfied, hung up the phone.

Then he picked up the telephone and dialed again.

"Hello La Regencia, this is Mr. Andros. I have a message for Mr. Lujack."

16

CONFRONTATION

LIVID, QUINTER DROVE SOUTH ON National Route 323. He thought about the coldly calculated manner in which Bordman lied to him and Jennifer, and conveniently overlooked a plot to murder them. His thoughts jumped to the emotional gut-wrenching he had endured as Jennifer was carried away against her will. And worse, he had been helpless to come to her aid.

Willing his anger to subside so he could think clearly, Quinter realized that Jennifer's ultimate safety might depend on his ability to remain a free agent. No one would consider silencing her so long as he remained at large. *No,* he thought, *I made the right decision—no matter how painful and humiliating.* And then he pounded the steering wheel with his fist in fury, welcoming the delicious sensation of pain that raced up his arm.

The well-paved road was wide and divided. Quinter checked his watch surprised that the time was only a quarter to 3:00. But he knew the intensity of events had unsettled his sense of time. Again, he pounded the steering wheel. "That bastard!" he said. "That no good bastard!"

The kilometers flew by as the scenic highway wound its way through the Sierra Nevada Mountains. A sign announced: "Almuñécar 35 kilometers." Quinter pressed forward.

JENNIFER SAT ON the large brass bed, alternately rubbing the handcuff marks on each of her wrists. She glanced through the open bedroom door toward the living room. One of her two captors sat on the sofa facing her and the other stood next to a chair.

"Why don't you go down to the restaurant and pick us up a couple of sandwiches," the young man with wavy black hair asked in Spanish. "Francisco and Taminos won't be back for another thirty or forty minutes. Aren't you hungry?"

"Can you handle her?" the older, gray-haired men asked in a slightly sarcastic way.

"No problem. Where would she go?" replied the younger man. But he took the small Beretta out of his holster and placed it on the table.

"Well, alright, I could eat something. I'll be back soon. Make sure she doesn't leave the bedroom."

Jennifer lost no time in seeing her chance. She turned her back to the door and, with her right hand unbuttoned her blouse so that the upper part of her breasts was visible. She reached in her purse, which had been returned to her, withdrew a little bottle of Chanel No.5, and shook some between her breasts, spreading it with her left hand.

With her hairbrush, she began brushing her hair using long slow strokes. With each stroke she arched her back and allowed her head to be pulled in the direction of the brush-strokes. After half a minute she looked to her left and was satisfied the man was watching. She smiled provocatively and turned her head away, rising from the bed and walking out of his view toward the tall mirror on the dressing table. Soon, she heard the man say in broken English from the doorway, "Señorita, please to remain where I can see you."

"Certainly, señor, as you wish," she replied in Spanish, as she turned from the mirror toward the door and the sound.

"Ah, you speak Spanish," the man replied, watching her appreciatively as she continued to preen herself.

Ignoring his observation, Jennifer asked, "Do you have a woman?"

"I have many women," he said smugly. "All the señoritas like Alfredo."

"It is easy to understand why," she said lowering her eyes and casually separating her blouse with the fingertips of her left hand showing her cleavage and then letting the material fall naturally into position.

"You are so good looking, Alfredo. I noticed you right away." She looked up and as his eyes met hers, she could see his lust.

"You are too kind, señorita, but all the ladies say Alfredo is too handsome," he said with a smirk.

Jennifer moved several steps back to the bed continuing to brush her hair slowly. She placed both her hands behind her head and shook her shoulders as she looked at him. "Do you like me?" she asked softly and innocently.

"You are a beautiful woman, señorita."

Jennifer placed her right foot on the edge of the bed and began rubbing her ankle. Slowly, she moved her hands over her calf and up toward her knee, moving the blue flowered skirt out of the way and exposing a well-shaped thigh. "Thank you, Alfredo," she replied. She grasped her thigh and she moved her hands up and down allowing herself to luxuriate in the first sensations of pleasure.

Fascinated by her every move, the man began to feel the tension of a growing erection. He made a first step through the doorway in which he had been standing and into the room. Jennifer threw her head back and with her left hand on her knee, stroked the inside of her thigh with the fingertips of her right hand, and at the end of each stroke making contact with the yellow silk panties immediately over her clitoris.

Thrusting her hips forward she moaned softly, "Oh Alfredo, it feels so good. I want it, Alfredo. I need it, Alfredo."

"Señorita," Alfredo said huskily, moving to her and placing his left hand on her right shoulder, "Alfredo will give you what you need."

Alfredo grasped her hands and raised her from the bed, taking her in his arms. Jennifer kissed the side of his neck and reaching around his body took hold of his buttocks drawing him close to her and slightly to her right. Alfredo felt the warm pressure of her body against his now bulging penis as she rhythmically pulled his hips toward her and then released the pressure.

Sensuously, Jennifer worked her right leg between Alfredo's legs, and raising her leg, increased the contact of her warm thigh against his groin. He opened his legs slightly as he began kissing her shoulders and then the upper part of her breasts.

"Oh Alfredo," she murmured, pulling his buttocks toward her and pressing her upper thigh against his crotch again. Giving in to his passion, he moved against her eagerly. Jennifer lowered her leg, and with all her strength, brought her knee up sharply into his crotch. Alfredo's world went black and he fell in a heap on the ground.

Jennifer quickly unsnapped the handcuffs from his belt pocket, locking one of them around his right ankle and the other to the heavy brass bar at the foot of the bed. Alfredo continued to whine and moan as red and black stars alternated across his field of vision and waves of convulsing nausea passed through his body.

Jennifer grabbed her purse, and ran to the hotel room door. After checking to make sure no one was in the corridor, she dashed down the hall to the stairwell.

LA REGENCIA WAS a luxury hotel located south of the Paseo de Priete Moreno, facing a stretch of rocky coast. A few hundred feet to the east, the coastline almost miraculously broadened into a wide sandy beach. To the west, the rugged Almuñécar peninsula jutted out into the sparkling blue sea.

Quinter walked through the lobby of the hotel to the registration desk. In no time, an efficient young woman with black hair tied in a bun came out to greet him.

"How long will you be staying with us?" she asked in English, sensing that Quinter would not be comfortable with Spanish.

"Only a night or so," Quinter replied. "The name's Andros. Do you have any messages for me?"

The receptionist checked and handed Quinter an envelope. It was addressed to "Mr. Andros," and he quickly tore it open.

"Tom," it read, "got your message about Jennifer. I've told Deacon. Back soon. Room 519. Keep your cool. She'll be O.K. Graham. 3:00 pm."

Quinter crumpled the paper and put it in his pocket. The receptionist handed him the room key, and he asked her for paper and an envelope. He walked across the lobby to a small mahogany writing desk and wrote: "Graham, received your note. Room 620. I'm going to put some heat on that son of a bitch Bordman. He can have Jenny released if he wants to, and I'm going to persuade him that he needs to do it immediately. Meet you here at about 7:00 pm—if all goes well. Quinter. 4:15 pm."

He closed the envelope, addressed it to "Mr. Lujack, Room 519," and gave the message to the desk clerk.

Quinter took the elevator to the sixth floor. Inside room 620, he threw his traveling bag on the bed, opened the blinds, and looked to the beach below where he could see people playing in the surf. He returned to the bed, and from his bag took out the shoulder holster with the Mauser inside.

He removed the gun, and taking a clip from the bag, snapped it into the grip. He then took another magazine and slipped it into the left inside breast pocket of his jacket on the bed. Putting on the holster, he adjusted it snugly, and then put on his jacket.

"Now it's time for a little chat, old friend," he said, bitterly. Quinter pulled the car keys from his pocket, and left the room.

Taking the back road, he approached Quinta de la Torre from the south, and parked the Seát a short distance from the villa. He walked up Torre Road until he came to the path leading up the stiff incline to La Torre. Within ten minutes, he was standing with his back to the tower looking down on La Herradura. The village appeared serene and calm, a marked contrast to the fury percolating inside him, and he focused his attention on the villa below. A single car was parked in the driveway, and the wooden door in the wall appeared to be slightly ajar.

He studied the scene for several minutes. Observing no activity he retraced his steps down the gravel path to Torre Road and walked the remaining distance to the villa.

The sun was still high in the late afternoon sky as Quinter pushed open the door to the grounds. He walked down the curving stone path toward the kitchen door and then around the corner of the house. He continued along the side of the villa passing by the side entrance toward the front of the house. When he reached the tile steps leading to the long front porch, he paused at the bottom, reached inside his jacket to unsnap the leather retaining strap, and withdrew the pistol. He chambered a round, put the gun in his right side pocket, and started up the steps.

As soon as his eyes were above the porch floor level, he saw Bordman, sitting with his back to the fountain and the orange trees, his feet on the low wall which followed the front edge of the porch. A tumbler filled with clear liquid and ice cubes sat on the glass-topped table next to the vodka bottle.

Quinter put his right hand in his pocket and took hold of the gun, snapping off the safety. Then he walked silently up the remaining steps, and started across the porch, keeping close to the front of the house and behind Bordman's line of sight. Passing the patio doors, he noticed there was no one in the living room or den. About twenty feet away he stopped as Bordman raised his glass to drink.

"You fuckin' bastard. You fuckin' bastard."

The sound of Quinter's voice startled Bordman. He jumped up from the chair and turned toward Quinter.

"Why Tom," he said, "you scared the hell out of me. Nice to see you." Bordman began walking toward Quinter his hand extended in greeting.

"That's close enough, asshole," said Quinter. "Politics ain't gonna get you nothing." He pulled the Mauser from his pocket and leveled it at Bordman's chest. "I'd love to blow a few holes in you just for enjoyment."

Bordman stopped, and held up his hands in front of him. The steel in Quinter's tone told him that if he moved he would be shot.

"You fed us to the wolves, you son of a bitch. Now, I want you to walk into the villa and make a telephone call. Move!"

Quinter placed his thumb on the hammer of the gun and pulled it back two clicks to firing position.

"All right, Tom, anything you say," said Bordman. Quinter followed him as he walked through the patio, past the fountain, and into the living room.

"Any of your friends here?"

"Just you and me, Tom."

"Good. Now, I want you to call your buddies at National Security and tell them to release Jennifer. If you do it right, maybe, just maybe I won't blow your fuckin' brains out. And don't tell them where you're calling from."

"O.K. O.K., but the number is in my wallet."

"Move slowly and keep your hands in sight. All I need is the slightest excuse."

From his wallet Bordman carefully withdrew a piece of paper. He picked up the telephone and dialed the number.

"Colonel Taminos, please, Dave Bordman calling."

A few seconds elapsed. "Good afternoon Colonel. I've been discussing the situation about the girl, Jennifer Millieux, with some of the Nortex people. Yes. We think you should release her. She can't do us any harm.

"What's that? She got away? Well, well, a very resourceful lady. Thank you Colonel. We'll be in touch."

Bordman hung up the telephone. "Jennifer escaped, Tom. National Security's upset about it."

Bordman turned toward Quinter, taking a small sip from the glass. "You see, Tom, things generally work out." And with a flick of his wrist, Bordman threw the drink, glass and all, in Quinter's face. The glass struck him on his nose and right cheek, and the liquid burned in Quinter's eyes. Simultaneously crouching and then springing up, Bordman knocked the pistol out of Quinter's hand with his left forearm. Quinter fell backward over the sofa.

In an instant Bordman was on him, and, with the heel of his hand, hammering his face and the right side of his neck with short powerful blows.

Quinter grabbed Bordman's hair, and rolled off the sofa dragging Bordman with him, smashing his head into the tile floor. Bordman was stunned. Quinter got up slowly to his full height, his senses reeling. Seeing Bordman moving on the floor, he jumped on him driving his right knee into the pit of Bordman's stomach. Bordman vomited immediately.

Quinter grabbed Bordman's hair and resumed smashing his head against the tile floor, again and again. Someone grabbed Quinter from behind, but he continued to drive Bordman's head into the floor, blood now flowing from Bordman's mouth and right ear.

"Tom! Tom! You're going to kill him. Stop. Tom. Stop it!"

Through a fog of rage and pain, Quinter recognized the voice of Graham Butler. He stopped smashing Bordman's head and allowed himself to be restrained.

"Jesus, Tom. I hope he's not dead. We need the son of a bitch."

Shaking uncontrollably, Quinter staggered to a chair across from where Bordman lay groaning and writhing, and fell sideways into the seat. Butler placed a sofa pillow under Bordman's head and handcuffed his hands in front of him. He walked over to the telephone and dialed.

"Deacon's Messenger Service, may I help you?"

"Mr. Richard Deacon, please. Graham Butler calling."

"Just a moment, Sir."

"Good afternoon Mr. Butler."

"Mr. Deacon, we've had a slight problem develop. Quinter and Bordman have had a confrontation. I've got Bordman secured here at the villa in La Herradura. He's messy, and needs immediate medical attention. Quinter's shaken, but he'll be all right."

Deacon replied, "We need to keep Bordman under wraps for twenty-four hours until after the reception party for the Star. We would prefer to take her when she docks in Malaga tomorrow rather than on the high seas. Wouldn't want that information circulated. Can we pick him up there? I can have a man on the scene in an hour."

"Pick another place for the exchange. His buddies could return any time," Butler responded.

"O.K. How about Almuñécar, the service parking lot behind La Regencia? You're staying there, right?"

"Yes, that's fine. 7:00? That's an hour and a half."

"Good. By the way, Mr. Butler, tell our hero one of my people is on his way to pick up Miss Millieux now. Seems she did a number on one of the young National Security lover boys. They're pretty embarrassed, though they do see a certain element of raw humor. She's fine. I'm bringing her to Almuñécar tonight. We'll arrive at the hotel about 8:00."

"I'll let him know. His room number is 620."

"And Butler, tell Quinter to keep the hell out of our affairs before he screws up something we can't fix."

"I'll tell him," said Butler, looking at Quinter who by now was almost prone in the chair. Seeing the nasty swelling that had already begun to engulf the entire right side of Quinter's face, Butler added, "But I really don't think he's much in the mood for action at the moment."

"Excellent. Keep him company. Good bye, Mr. Butler."

Butler hung up the telephone. "Come on, Tom. Let's get this bastard Bordman out of here."

17

A Reception at Seventeen West

Quinter lay on his bed in the hotel room. There was a half-eaten bowl of cold chicken soup and an empty glass of milk on the bedside table. He ached all over, and it was painful for him to apply the ice, which Butler had wrapped in a towel, to the swelling on the right side of his neck and face. He closed his eyes and grimaced.

"Hurts, huh, Buddy?" said Butler who was sitting in the chair behind the small writing table.

Quinter simply grunted. He started to roll over on his left side, but was abruptly stopped by a searing pain on the left side of his back, which he'd wrenched when Bordman had driven him over the sofa.

A knock on the door was followed by the announcement, "Richard Deacon and friend."

Butler, who'd been made anxious by the sound, relaxed, and walked over to open the door.

Jennifer entered, followed by Deacon. With difficulty Quinter pulled himself to a sitting position, and Jennifer came quickly to his side.

"You poor man. You look terrible." She sat down on the bed next to him and took his hands in hers.

Quinter studied her closely. She was not the same person who had boarded the Nortex Gates Learjet with him at Lakefront airport in Cleveland an eternity ago. She seemed sure of herself, more confident, somehow more in control.

"I missed you," Quinter began. "I was afraid that they would . . ."

"Shush, honey," she interrupted as she put her right hand lightly over his lips silencing him, and kissed him on the forehead.

Butler turned to Deacon. "I don't think we're needed any longer."

"Don't think so. Mr. Quinter, you have a 3:00 o'clock flight from Malaga to Madrid tomorrow. Miss Millieux has all the details and the tickets. But, to sum it up, you'll be picked up at Barajas International by Embassy staff. They'll want to ask you some questions and will keep you overnight, prior to departure for Washington. I guess some Senator on the Armed Forces Committee wants to talk to you. Glad things worked out for you Mr. Quinter. You too, Miss Millieux. Come on Butler. You and I must set the table for a party tomorrow."

"What about Bordman?" interjected Quinter.

"Oh, Bordman," replied Deacon. "He's in an Air Force hospital outside Almeria about two hundred kilometers east of here. You broke his skull in several places, but the fractures are linear and he'll be all right in a week or so. His real problems haven't even begun. Wait until the Justice Department gets through with him and Nortex. So long."

Deacon walked over to the door and, followed by Butler, left the room. As Butler reached the doorway, he paused, turned toward the couple, smiled, and tipped his right hand to his forehead in an informal salute of admiration.

Jennifer glanced down at Quinter. His eyes were closed and he was breathing the first regular deep breaths of deep sleep.

"We'll make our own party," she murmured, "lots of them, my love."

COMMANDER BESSIMER SMITH stood on the bridge of the USS frigate Scorpion scanning the flat Mediterranean Sea over the five-inch forward deck guns. The moon was bright in the cloudless sky and the ship bobbed gently as she rode the long swells. The night air was soft and the only breeze was that generated by the slow forward motion of the Scorpion. The low thrum of her diesels provided the sole sound. Off the port side, Smith glanced at the ship he had been shadowing for twelve hours.

The Scorpion had been at sea for five months with only the occasional port of call, and Commander Smith was looking forward to some rest and relaxation in Mallorca. *Yes, ten days in Mallorca would be just fine.*

His first officer interrupted his thoughts.

"Message from OP-INTELL-PAC, Sir. They want to know an estimated time of arrival for the tanker in Malaga."

The Commander looked at the luminescent dial of his military watch. *02:00 hours,* he thought. *That should put the Star in port about 11:30 tomorrow morning.*

"Very well, Lieutenant," he said, "Get Navigation on the calculation and report back."

205

"Aye, Sir. And if she passes port, they want us to board her."

"Understood, Lieutenant," responded Commander Smith, waiving the junior officer off with a crisp salute.

Ah, thought Smith returning to his reverie, *Mallorca will be just fine.*

QUINTER WAS AWAKENED by a jolt of pain in his neck. For a few seconds he didn't recognize the surroundings, but then saw Jennifer sitting out on the balcony reading the paper. The sun was well up in the sky. He got up slowly, testing each movement and finding, to his satisfaction, that most of his body worked reasonably well. Halfway to the balcony, he had to steady himself on the chair behind the writing table. He called Jennifer's name.

"Gee honey," she answered. "aren't you beautiful?"

Quinter limped over to the full-length mirror. The right side of his face was swollen and had already begun turning the first light shades of a blue-blackish green. A scab was beginning to form over the cut on the right side of his mouth.

"No beauty prize for me, huh, honey? What time is it?"

"8:30. You slept for twelve hours. How do you feel?"

"I'll be all right," he answered, stoically but genuinely.

Within an hour, Quinter and Jennifer were headed west on National Route 340 toward Malaga. In accordance with Deacon's instructions, with Jennifer driving Butler's Green Volkswagen, they reached the beginning of the long descent into the center of the city. They had not spoken much on the trip, during most of which Quinter had slept fitfully. But now he was awake and his gaze came to rest on the city glistening in the forenoon sun below.

"Jenny, we've got some time before the flight. Let's go take a look at Seventeen West. We will pass right by the port."

"Thomas Quinter," she responded in a mock scolding tone of voice, "Deacon told you that you had to let the issue drop. It's their business now."

"I know," he answered in a forlorn manner, "but there'd be no harm in just a look. I have my binoculars . . ."

"I suppose we could take a quick look," she replied.

Jennifer drove through the city and at the westerly edge, proceeded northwest up into the low foothills. Gauging the distance by the relative position of the waterfront below, she brought the car to a stop off the edge of the two lane country road.

Quinter took his binoculars from the case, and they walked up the road for a hundred feet until they came to an outcropping of flat brown rocks on the north side of the road. They clambered up to a vantage point from which they had an excellent view of the city, the surrounding countryside, and the sea. Quinter took his binoculars and for a minute scanned the sea.

"Look Jenny," he said, with a note of triumph, "there she is. The *Middle Eastern Star*. About three or four miles out and making for port. And there's a navy ship about four or five miles behind her to the south."

Quinter handed her the glasses.

"I see them," she said in an excited voice.

S ERGEANT DELLANZO WALKED slowly out toward the end of Seventeen West, enjoying the warmth of the sun on his shoulders. He was disappointed that the National Security Police had excluded him from the exciting work in Granada, but surely this señor Taminos would keep his promise and make a complimentary entry in his file. In any event, he felt good that he had spotted the car and followed the vehicle through the hills without being detected.

He looked out across the harbor, and saw the great tanker, a half a mile distant, slowly maneuvering into docking position. *This is the only dockage between Gibraltar and Cartagena that could handle such a ship*, he thought to himself, and then adding proudly, *and I am chief of security at Seventeen West!*

Dellanzo continued to watch the vessel while the harbor pilot skillfully positioned it stern first for final docking procedures. As dockhands took their places, the pier came alive with activity. When the port side touched the large rubber bumpers, members of the ship's crew heaved lines to the dock workers, and, in short order, the vessel was made fast.

Quinter watched as the Star berthed. His nervous apprehension turned to relief when he saw a column of National Security Police cars and trucks traveling up the Port road toward Seventeen West.

"Ah," he said as he turned to Jennifer, "I think the reception party is arriving. Look at all those vehicles, and the men in battle gear in the trucks. They have a damn army."

Sergeant Dellanzo returned to the guardhouse as the column of vehicles, led by a black BMW, pulled up to his gate. The driver walked rapidly toward the guardhouse, and Dellanzo met him at the open door.

"Sergeant Dellanzo!" the man said in recognition, "I'm Taminos of National Security. We meet again."

"Yes Sir," said Dellanzo coming to attention. "I remember you, Sir."

"We have orders to search the ship, Sergeant. The *Middle Eastern Star*, I believe?"

"Yes Sir."

"Well, Sergeant, we will be about our business. Here is the warrant. And, I haven't forgotten your report."

"Thank you, Sir. And Patrolman Dunsos too?"

"Patrolman Dunsos also."

Taminos flipped a brusque, very proper salute to Dellanzo, and returned to the car, closing the door behind him.

"Everything is in order, Mr. Deacon," Taminos said to the passenger in the left rear seat.

"Yes, it appears so," replied Deacon who then turned to the other rear seat passenger saying, "It does seem to be a fine day for a party, don't you think Mr. Butler?"

The BMW led the column up to the pier and came to rest. Taminos picked up the microphone and setting it to the tactical frequency pushed the key.

"Lieutenant, board her and search her from bow to stern."

"Yes Sir, we're on our way."

Deacon and Butler watched as the soldiers jumped from the trucks and the National Security Police poured from their cars, and then scampered up the gangway to the deck above. Shortly, the Lieutenant returned to the BMW.

"We found them sir. Tanks. Fifty M-1 tanks. We're taking pictures now."

"Very good, Lieutenant. Secure the ship and hold the crew for interrogation."

"Yes sir," replied the Lieutenant as he left the vehicle.

"Mr. Butler," Deacon said, "that was a fine reception."

"Yes," responded Butler, "but I have this lingering wish that Quinter could have seen the show."

"I think they've got them, Jenny," said Quinter while replacing the binoculars in the case. "I can't think of any other reason why they'd be taking pictures. Let's head for the airport. I'm hungry."

"I think you're feeling better," she said offering him her hand, and when he grasped it, helped him to his feet. "yes, my Love, let's go."

EPILOGUE

Quinter and Jennifer sat at a table next to a window on the Public Square side of the lobby of Stouffer's Hotel in Terminal Tower. The hotel's proclaimed 'Finest Sunday Morning Brunch in Town' was in full swing, and Quinter had helped himself to generous portions of scrambled eggs, potatoes, sausage, and various fruits including his favorite, red raspberries. He looked out at the fountain and watched the water cascade from step to step shimmering under the bright sun until it reached the pool at the base. A young couple sat on the pool's low half-moon wall, their feet in the moving water.

"The sign," he cried out, "where's the stupid sign?"

"What sign, honey?" asked Jennifer as she began to cut through a piece of cantaloupe with her table knife."

"The 'DANGER, DO NOT WADE' sign has been removed from the fountain," he replied forcefully. "Well, that's progress. Maybe we can make this a 'people' town after all."

"It always has been, Tom. It just depends upon the people and their attitude," she replied philosophically, keeping her attention fixed on the obstreperous melon which on two occasions had defeated her attempts to subdivide it.

"Now take us for example," she said, looking up and observing that the right side of his face had essentially returned to normal,

"We've made this a pretty good people place for ourselves."

"True," he answered, noticing, with no little pride, the sparkle of the diamond on her hand, "I guess I was registering a complaint about the way the bureaucracy cuts through our lives. I mean rules develop their own momentum, and after a while no one gives any thought to the effect they have on people. It's just a rule because it's a rule, and the fact of the rule becomes its justification."

Jennifer attacked the melon with renewed vigor. "You can't spend forever re-examining the basis for every decision," she said quietly as the melon surrendered. "the day's not long enough."

"Someone should," he answered with conviction. "That's how an enlightened society should operate. If the rule becomes the reason then no one will inquire about the right or wrong of it."

Quinter looked out at the fountain again. He hoped that the sign had been intentionally removed by the City and not just taken down by a vandal in the dark.

Moments later, his mind wandered back to last week when he and Jennifer had met with Senator James in his Washington office.

"MR. QUINTER, MISS Millieux," the Senator had begun sonorously, while shaking Quinter's hand, "we all owe you a debt of gratitude. This is Mr. Edwards of the CIA and Mr. Barber of the Department of Justice. I'm sure you remember Mr. Deacon. Please, please, have a seat."

The Senator motioned them to a plush overstuffed sofa at the side of the room across from his huge mahogany desk.

"I have some pictures that no doubt will interest you," he said, pulling several eight-by-ten color photographs from a manila file on his desk and handing them to Quinter. The first photograph showed an overall view of the bow of a tanker with the name '*Middle Eastern Star*' clearly visible. Several of the pictures were various shots of the deck and the superstructure. Others showed part of the warehouse and the pier of the dock. The remaining photographs showed the cargo hold with its rows of M-1 tanks and crates of unloaded goods.

"These, of course," the Senator said while pointing to the tanks with a flourish, "were not supposed to be part of the shipment to the Spanish Government. We got the *Star* in Malaga. Somehow, the *Crescent* slipped through the Suez, but the Navy took her just outside the Straits of Hormuz. Edwards, can you fill in Mr. Quinter and Miss Millieux?"

"Certainly Senator," Edwards replied. "it seems a rump group of the Nortex organization cut a deal with the Iranians to deliver the tanks in exchange for shipments of crude oil. Illegal and contrary to United States policy, of course. But these clever folks had by-passed regular production procedures by reprogramming inventory levels and the computer's reporting function. Obviously, they had a man on the inside, but as yet we've not been able to identify that individual. If the goods hadn't been discovered and stopped in transit, we might never have uncovered the deal."

Quinter had been listening intently, anger building. "'Rump group,' you say! 'Rump group', my ass! This charade had the full support of the Nortex organization right up to the highest levels!"

"Well," Edwards had continued, "we do know there was heavy involvement of the Energia Division, and, of course, your 'friend', Bordman. But . . ."

Senator James, who had sat down in the chair behind his desk, interrupted. "Now, we don't want to jump to any conclusions, Tom. I have Mr. Johnson's personal assurance the matter will be the subject of an immediate and thorough corporate investigation, and the Department of Justice, Mr. Barber," the Senator gestured toward the blue pin-stripe-suited Mr. Barber, "can expect the fullest co-operation. All participants will be subject to involuntary dismissal and prosecution to the fullest extent of the law."

"Including his son?" Quinter had interjected, his voice dripping with sarcasm.

"Well, Joel—Mr. Johnson told me privately that Joel was taken in by these, these international outlaws. We'll investigate, of course, but even at this early stage, it's clear to me the ringleader was this Bordman fellow."

"Bullshit," Quinter had said almost inaudibly.

"Excuse me?" the Senator had said.

"I said bullshit!" Quinter repeated the word loudly enough to be heard in the outer office.

"Motivated by pure personal greed," Quinter all but shouted, "Johnson and his cronies orchestrated this entire mess. Those are the people you ought to be going after. Except for David Bordman, the people you're looking at are pawns."

Quinter stared at Deacon who stared back at him blankly.

"Well, Tom and Jennifer—may I call you Jennifer?—you must be tired," the Senator had said as he got up from his desk and walked over toward them seated on the sofa. "We've got a wonderful place for you to spend the evening before we fly you back to Cleveland . . . is it Cleveland? Yes, Cleveland, fine town . . . in the morning."

Jennifer and Quinter rose as the Senator added, "Yes, and fine job. The American people owe you a debt of gratitude. I wouldn't be surprised if the President himself wouldn't like to meet you after he receives our report. You have the Country's deepest appreciation."

Senator James, who had been walking the couple out through the outer office, now stood framed in the entrance door, his right hand extended, indicating the meeting was over.

"Take care, folks," he said, his face frozen in his very well-practiced smile.

"Tom, check this out," said Jennifer, startling Quinter back to the reality of Sunday morning at Stouffer's. She handed him the first section of the Sunday *New York Times*. In the lower right corner there was a short article.

"NORTEX UNCOVERS ILLEGAL SALES. Madrid. Nortex Corporation spokesman Joel Johnson announced today the company uncovered a scheme by mid-level employees to send an arms shipment to a participant in the Middle East conflict. According to Mr. Johnson, an investigation is underway and the company is working closely with the Department of Justice and appropriate congressional committees."

"Unbelievable." sighed Quinter. "Those snakes got away with it, and now they're going to get away with a cover-up. Damn it, Jenny, I can't let this happen!"

"I know you can't, honey, and whatever you do, I'll be with you. But for right now, this moment, let's go stick our feet in the fountain."